Relative Distances

RELATIVE DISTANCES

Victoria Jenkins

PEREGRINE SMITH BOOKS
SALT LAKE CITY

First edition

93 92 91 90   4 3 2 1

This is a Peregrine Smith Book,
published by Gibbs Smith, Publisher,
P.O. Box 667, Layton, Utah 84041

All characters in this work are purely
fictional and any resemblance to any
person, living or dead, is purely
coincidental

Design by J. Scott Knudsen, Park City,
Utah

Cover illustration by Howard Post

Manufactured in the United States of
America

**Library of Congress
Cataloging-in-Publication Data**

Jenkins, Victoria,
   Relative distances / Victoria Jenkins
      p.   cm.
   ISBN 0-87905-251-1
   I. Title.
PS3560.E514R45   1990
813'.54—dc20   90-7042
                                    CIP

The paper used in this publication
meets the minimum requirements of
the American National Standard for
Information Sciences—Permanence of
Paper for Printed Library Materials,
ANSI Z39.48-1984 ∞

For my friends in Platte and Converse counties

Chapter One

Myra Wells stood in the mine office after her shift and forfeited a week's pay in lieu of notice. She let the foreman pour a farewell shot of George Dickel into her coffee and keep his arm around her shoulders while he walked her to the door when the van honked outside. He was sorry to lose her, and she suddenly felt treasured and foolish and would have surrendered if he'd asked her to stay on, but the bourbon and the embrace were the only liberties he took, and he didn't ask.

She turned from the frontage road, her car, an old Cadillac, relic of a past romance, finned, red under layers of highway sprayed slush, surging on tired suspension as it bucked the ruts at the entrance to a trailer park and nosed between chevron rows of mobile homes—the whole prairie to spread out on but clustered here in tight symmetry like wagons drawn into a circle. Smoke from a smoldering trash barrel angled eastward and pasted ash against the windshield like grimy snow. Dogs announced her passing. She pulled in beside an old Airstream once painted camouflage green but peeling

now to show the aluminum beneath, set up on railroad
ties and anchored to its space by a clothesline tethered
to the neighbor. Blue jeans and long johns flapped stiffly
in the wind.

At the back of the trailer she set a jack on a flat place
she kicked into snow that had melted and refrozen. She
pumped the handle and the trailer rose and swayed. The
door was flung open, banging back against the side in
the wind, and Vernon catapulted out. He skidded
around the back of the trailer in his socks, shirttails flapping, and came up short when he saw Myra. He
hunched his shoulders against the wind and tucked his
hands into his armpits.

Myra looked up at him. "Hi, Vernon," she said, and
went back to pumping the jack. "I'm leaving." She
glanced back at him and watched the effort to catch up
with her and his rejection of her meaning chase across
his face. He was jigging a little in the cold.

"Shoot, honey, where're we going?"

Myra straightened up and looked into his face. "I'm
going alone, Vernon." She saw the protest dawning and
spoke again, turning away, back to the jack. "I'm sorry,
honey. I never meant to hurt you." She paused. "But
I'm going." She pushed the railroad ties with her foot.
They didn't give and she leaned again on the jack handle. She glanced at him as she spoke, gauging his reac-
tion. "I'm thirty-six this year. That's halfway through,
you know." She stopped again and waved her arm at the
row of trailers, getting shrill, "I don't want to be here.
Doing this. Working for the mine."

"But Myra . . . ," he said, and stopped, not having
framed the rest of his thought.

"Vernon, you knew this wasn't forever. We've had
some fun. Don't let's get all mournful about it." The
weight was off the ties and Myra pushed the top one
and it toppled off and she grasped its end and pulled it
from underneath the trailer. She straightened and looked
at her hands, then at Vernon again. "It's not you, Vernon, and I'm not mad. I just want to move on." She

dropped down in the snow and pulled herself under the
trailer on her back and changed the waste hookup over
to the holding tank, using both hands to unscrew the
length of plastic pipe. When she slid back out beside his
stockinged feet she had to cough as she sat up to cover a
smile. He was sweet enough, or could be, but from the
first when she'd hooked up with him it hadn't been
something she figured would last forever. Nothing did,
Myra thought, just longer or shorter, but not for good,
not for her anyway. You couldn't get something between two people down, give it a wrap and a hooey,
and expect it to stay put for life.

He followed her, cold and speechless, as she freed
the trailer from the water and electricity, kneeing away
insulating bales of sodden hay, and pulled the remaining
tie from under the back of the trailer. She let the jack
down and the trailer's weight sighed onto the tires.

Myra got into her car, started it, and pulled forward,
then maneuvered back again, craning over her shoulder.
Vernon stood by the fender and guided her with small
reflexive movements of his hand, unconsciously abetting
her going. She got out and wound the front of the trailer
up until the weight was off the other set of ties, then
dragged them free and lowered the trailer onto the
hitch. Gently, as she might remind a child, Myra said,
"You want anything from inside, Vernon?"

He looked blankly at her for a moment then stepped
over the trailer hitch and went around the corner and
in.

Myra cut the clothesline where it was tied to a screw
eye in the side of the trailer and gathered the clothes
still hanging from it into a stiff bundle as she walked
toward the neighboring trailer. She knocked, and the
door opened. Blue light from a television flickered into
the dusk. Myra held out the armload of clothes. "Here's
your wash. I'm pulling out."

Behind her Vernon stepped out of her trailer, wearing a jacket now and an Exxon cap, his Adidas untied, a
pillowcase serving as a suitcase in one hand, a pair of

boots under his arm, and a bunch of shirts on hangers in the other hand. The neighbor's door closed, leaving them in darkness.

"You're a bitch, Myra," said Vernon.

This made her smile. "I know. And you're not the first man to tell me."

Vernon opened the door of his pickup and threw his stuff inside. His surprise was wearing off. He followed Myra as she went around to the driver's side of the Cadillac and grabbed her and swung her around. He shook her roughly, holding both her arms. "You can't just leave."

Myra tried to jerk free. "You watch," she said, scuffling like a girl, twisting against him to pull free, laughing.

Vernon let go and hit her with the back of his hand, getting her high up on the eyebrow as she ducked. She pulled loose of his other hand and slid into the car and slammed the door. Vernon leaned on the door and shouted in at her through an angled opening where the window wouldn't close, justifying himself, pleading. "What I can't stand is you won't even talk to me. Say why. You never even thought about how I was going to feel."

Myra looked through the glass at him, gone from him as though miles already intervened, oppressed by his importuning, but wishing with a detached tenderness to console. She touched her eyebrow and smiled. "I'll remember you for more than a few days, Vernon. 'Bye, darling. Good luck." She started the engine and stepped on the gas. The tires spun up a storm of red mud and slush. Vernon clung to the door as though he could hold her back. She gunned it and the car and trailer lurched away, sliding and fishtailing, pulling out of his grasp.

She turned from the four-lane at Sinclair and headed north, tunneling through the darkness. Later she pulled off the road into the barrow pit, and crawled into bed in

the trailer with her clothes on, and slept fitfully until
dawn.

Chapter Two

Myra parked in the ditch along the county road by a gate left lying open in the snow.. She got out and sat on the tilted fender and watched a pickup creep slowly across a wide expanse of bottom-land bounded on either side by ridges. A creek fringed with cottonwoods cut through the meadow, running clear and fast between scalloped rims of ice.

She had filled her tank at the Town Pump and asked the bored cashier with blue mottled arms for directions. She thought it must be Tom below in the meadow, standing on the tailgate flaking bales out onto the snow as the truck crept along. She heard his hoarse, mooing call carried on the wind, "Here boss, here boss. Boss, boss, boss. . . ." Cows, heavy with calves, their bellies swaying, broke from the red haze of willows along the creek and lumbered at an eager trot toward the truck.

Myra's heart raced when the pickup turned and passed slowly back along the line of hay and feeding cattle, then picked up speed as it wound up the hill toward her. She slid off the fender and leaned against the car, her hands in her pockets. The wind blew her hair across her face.

He was riding in the back of the pickup, and as he
jumped down to close the gate he saw her and was arrested in the crouch of his landing, his hand on the rim
of the truck's bed. He straightened slowly. His face gave
nothing away. They stood in silence and his eyes shifted
away, then came back to her.

"Hi, Tom," she said, and took her hands from her
pockets. He stayed as he was and made her come to
him. She reached to hug him and felt his rounded
shoulders under his jacket, and smelled the familiar
musk of Copenhagen. She felt herself smaller than he,
her breasts flattening against his chest, and the feel of
him, grown now, a man, was unnerving. Her hair caught
in the roughness of his cheek.

He stood passively in her arms and said softly past
her ear, "Hi, Ma."

Myra dropped her arms and stepped back. "Me and
Vernon split up," she said.

He smiled faintly and his eyes narrowed. He walked
away from her and picked the gate up. "Who's Vernon?" he called to her as he closed it.

Myra's cheeks went suddenly hot with the shame of
his not knowing. She looked around and her eyes got
unexpectedly tangled up in the look from the boy waiting inside the pickup. A man really, like Tom—grown.
Arlen's boy, she supposed, whose name she couldn't
remember. Her hand went to her face, holding back her
hair in the wind, and she turned away and shrugged. "It
doesn't matter," she said as Tom came back to her. "I
guess it's been longer than I thought." They stood again
in silence until Myra said, "Let's go for a ride, honey,"
looking up at him, afraid he would refuse.

Tom opened the pickup door and said into it, "I'm
going with her. See you later."

"Who is that?" Neal asked, leaning across the seat to
catch the door before it slammed, but Tom had turned
and was sliding into the Cadillac beside Myra. Neal

pulled out and drove slowly on down the road, watching the car in the rearview mirror as it turned around at the gate, taking plenty of maneuvering to do it, and disappeared over the crest of the hill. Neal went with it in imagination: soft, red leather seats, smell of stale smoke, a daytime snort from a pint in the glove box, wind and road noise sealed away, and Tom—so much deeper than supposed to have such a possibility and never mention her—beside her.

Neal turned from the county road at the mailbox and switchbacked down the ridge to the ranch buildings grouped in a wide bend of the river. He pulled to a stop by an auto gate in a pole fence. Beyond were corrals, ankle deep in mud and standing water. A few horses looked up from a hayrack with wary interest when he got out.

Arlen came out of the slab-sided barn, pitched forward in a headlong walk, bloody to the elbows, and plunged his arms into a watering trough. Neal watched him through the fence. "Old Rollerskate's heifer calved," Arlen said, and Neal smiled, thinking of the big, black cow with tits dragging. Arlen shook water from his arms and rolled down his sleeves. "Where's Tom?"

Neal had known he'd ask. "He went to town."

This swung Arlen around. "Why, for Christ's sake?"

"I don't know. He just did," said Neal, allying himself with Tom.

"I can't believe it." Arlen was shouting now, arms waving. "You boys. We're in the middle of calving and you take off and go to town. You two together don't make one good hand."

"If you look close you'll see I'm not in town," Neal said mildly.

"Catch up a horse and take those three that calved last night down to the meadow and check on the others," said Arlen, and stamped back into the barn.

You could never have the last word, Neal thought. Or if you did, you might as well not, because he wouldn't hear it.

Neal stood in the mud of the corral, a halter rope concealed behind his back. A thin bay horse faced him, feet
spread, ready to leap away in any direction, its neck a
tense arc. "Clay, you old rip, I'm not going to hurt
you," his voice a caress. "Easy boy. Come on." He took
one slow step toward the horse and it twitched and
swung its head but didn't jump away. "You old fool.
Easy now."

Arlen came to the door of the barn and watched
Neal in the corral for a minute. Then he shouted, "Neal,
for God's sake, take a horse you can catch. That's a fool
waste of time, messing with that horse."

At the sound of the voice the horse leapt away. Neal
stood for a moment, letting the rope hang down, looking at his feet in the mud. He might have had him that
time. Then he sighed and looked at the other horses
watching him with their eyes and ears, waiting for a
sixth sense to telegraph his choice. The fat pinto he and
Bonnie had ridden as kids laid back her ears at his first
step. Neal slipped the rope around her neck, and in a
few minutes rode off bareback behind the heifers and
their new, wobbling calves, loose and curved, feet dangling, his dignity abandoned, though Arlen was nowhere
to see and despair.

At supper that night the four of them ate in silence, their
heads bowed over their plates. Arlen's anger at the missing Tom punished them all. Florence was up and down
between the stove and the table. Then lights wheeled
outside as a car rounded the corner coming down the
hill from the county road, and Neal knew immediately it
was the Cadillac by its low, powerful, slightly liquid
rumble that set off a sympathetic quiver somewhere in
his center. No one reacted but he knew they were listening to the sound of the engine, straining for recognition,
and it gave him a tiny prick of pleasure to know they
could never guess. He went on eating. There was stillness outside, then the thud of the car door. The lights

swept past the porch, illuminated the trees in the yard
and the wall of the shop, then receded and disappeared
up the hill.

Tom stepped into the porch and hung his cap and
jacket, then came into the kitchen. Florence handed him
a plate as he passed and Bonnie smirked up at him with
a full mouth. Arlen kept his attention on his plate. Tom
sat down and helped himself. His eyes met Neal's across
the silent table, questioning, where did he stand? He
looked down and started to eat quickly.

Arlen pushed his plate away and tipped back in his
chair, rubbing his head. "Where in the hell did you take
off to?" Tom looked up and laid his fork down. He kept
his gaze fixed on Arlen's face. "You come sliding in here
in time for your meals but you're not around when
there's work that needs done." He got up and walked
around the kitchen, his hand stuck in the back of his
pants to ease a chronic ache. Neal watched him. He'd
taken his boots off and padded in his socks, hardly taller
than Florence, but he turned and shouted at Tom as
though undiminished. "Jesus. I ought to fire you. I
would if I wasn't already shorthanded."

Neal watched him with Tom's eyes—a ranting ban-
tam, shouting untruths to coerce an explanation that
Tom would stubbornly refuse to offer—and was
ashamed, and forgave his exclusion from the afternoon.

"Well?" said Arlen.

"I'll make it up to you. I'm sorry," Tom said softly.
Their eyes held in a skirmish Arlen couldn't win. He
grunted and picked the newspaper up off the washing
machine and sat down again and opened it on top of his
plate.

Florence leaned over Tom and poured him a cup of
coffee, her hand, gently laid on his shoulder, coercion
of another sort. "Who brought you back just now?"

Tom looked up and his eyes flickered around the
room. He took a gulp of coffee, mopped his plate with a
piece of bread and fitted half of it into his mouth, then
stood up and mumbled through his mouthful, "Myra."

Her name was like a stone tossed into a pool, sinking, while eyes flew from face to face in an instant of disclosure before their silence closed over it.

Chapter Three

Myra. It had been years and years since Arlen had seen her, and she didn't cross his mind much anymore—though she used to—but even so, and Valerie Pruitt not withstanding, the thought of her now stopped his heart. He had seldom thought of Myra as Tom's mother and the reminder that she was caught him up—claims on her from another quarter. He had a thousand memories of her, and of his thoughts of her, from the years when her image was forever before him. He thought he'd like to see her now, not needing her or wanting her, caring more for Valerie, because through all the years his passion for her had wrestled with his will to reject her and had tied him in knots, and now he thought he could see her without the inward struggle with desire. He'd like to punish her with his indifference. Questions came winging up in his mind, but Tom was already gone, and he couldn't have asked anyway. Where was she? Was she staying? How did she look? Did she ever think of him? He thought of her as she'd always looked to him: a calm, charged column he ached to touch and possess, standing before him, bringing him down with her siren's smile.

He felt Florence's eyes on him and looked at her, and caught in her glance a tender scorn mixed with fear. How could she fear his thoughts of Myra when he was already so lost to her? She wore one of his faded flannel shirts with the untucked tail ruckled high around her cushiony hips. It was a long time since he'd laid his hand on her pony's rump and he had a sudden impulse to reach out and pat her now.

He wished he'd gone to the door when the car pulled in and flicked on the floodlight hung in the cottonwood and pinned Myra in its scrutiny.

Tom was gone before Neal's mind caught up with what he'd said. Myra. Cousin Myra. Tom's mother. Jesus Christ. He thought back to the afternoon up on the road and the woman by the car in the wind. He'd known she was older, but not like that. Not enough to be Tom's mother, and besides, he would never have guessed she was anyone's mother. Her eyes had caught his for only a moment but he'd felt they'd shared something. Her look had gone straight to his heart. He'd held that moment in his mind, knowing it was there, knowing he'd come back to it later and turn it over and prize it, and now it was all turned to confusion. He'd had a woman in his mind, had thought she was real, and now one word told him he'd created her—the woman on the road was someone else. The loss was a weight spiraling down in his mind. The picture of her, the wind whipping her hair and her eyes meeting his then lifting to Tom's face, had buoyed his spirits during the afternoon—a little bubble of lightness that, God knew, he needed. He hadn't thought beyond that image, though he knew he would have later, when he'd had time, and now . . . it was cousin Myra.

He'd heard about her all his life, and guessed he'd seen her from time to time when he was little, but he didn't remember. Nobody talked about her much anymore, the Dyers were so scattered and splintered by squabbles. Tom had never mentioned her.

Neal got up and helped his mother clear the table. Except for the rattle of the dishes the kitchen was silent. It was always that way—silence or shouting. He wanted to get out. He scraped the plates and stepped through the porch and outside.

The dogs were immediately before him, tongues hanging. He put the scraps down for them. The wind was rushing in the big cottonwoods in the yard. He went back into the porch and got his cap and jacket and went out again. The door banged behind him.

The road was rutted and muddy with a frozen crust that gave stiffly beneath his boots. He walked past the shop, teetered across the auto gate, and continued past the calving barn to the horse corral. He climbed the fence and sat for a moment on the top pole. There was just enough light bouncing between old snow and the low cloud ceiling for him to make out the horses across the corral at the hayrack. He jumped down lightly. There was a thin skin of ice over the standing puddles and he felt the wet and chill penetrate his boots. He regretted his overshoes left lying in the porch. The horses blew softly and swung their heads but went on eating as he squished toward them. Except Clay. He snorted, backed away from the others, and jumped sideways away from Neal's approach with a sucking splash, and trotted along the fence with an airborne grace, each hoof suspended in a moment of impulsion before returning to the mud. Neal followed him, angling across the corral to pin him in the corner of the fence. Clay came to the angle and bunched himself, head up, seeing Neal coming behind him. He whirled and leaped, but Neal flung out his arms, and Clay stopped and backed up until his haunches wedged in the corner, forefeet braced and neck arced. Neal stopped too and stood before him, murmuring. In the dark the horse had a warm, electric aura, imperceptible in daylight.

Neal often visited Clay like this, longing to win the horse with his good will. Once caught, Clay was fine, smooth and supple, head outstretched on a loose rein, though green as grass. It was the catching of him that was so hard. He had to be roped. They had tried leaving him haltered but always at the last instant he'd jerk away. It was maddening that he never learned, never accepted the inevitability of his capture, and persisted in eluding every effort until finally he couldn't escape the sailing circle of rope. He fought fiercely at first, sitting back and flinging himself about, head up and chin in the air, one eye looking down his nose in dread. This would have been nothing to Arlen if it hadn't been for Neal crooning there in the corral, turning up an underbelly of softness that Arlen was compelled to poke.

Neal held out his hand, stretching his arm toward Clay, and felt his breath in tremulous columns against his palm. Then the horse exploded along the fence line. Neal had not touched him and he was gone.

Neal turned around in disappointment and slogged back across the corral. He climbed the fence and walked back to the calving barn, slid the door open and looked in. A light was left on. The heifers stood against the wall on the far side of the barn. They looked at him as he entered, and he stood by the door and watched them watching him. Poor fools, two years old, not fully grown themselves, yet about to become mothers. Their bags were small and tight and their frames compact. They looked at him with a cheerful, mindless anticipation. One of the heifers had a hump in her back and her tail was out, and Neal hunkered by the door to wait in case she needed help.

The heifers saddened him. They always did. He liked the cows, liked their bulk and warmth and low voices— liked their competence. They lay down in the field and gave birth and licked the calf clean and dry and suckled it, and swung around with a protective, alert energy at the approach of a dog or man. But the heifers were crazy and unpredictable, often not recognizing that they

had become mothers and rejecting their calves, getting
up from the straw and never even turning to sniff the
steaming, slippery, helpless spark of life they had ex-
pelled, kicking the calf away from its attempts to nurse.
Then it was a fight, drying the calf roughly with burlap
bags, cleaning its nostrils and throat of stringy, choking
mucous, hurrying, tying up the mother, hobbling her,
helping the calf to suck and hoping that the heifer
would come to her senses. The instinct and capability
for maternity had been bred out of them. Sometimes the
calf would have to be snagged by a man thrusting
shoulder deep into the heifer with a chain to wrap
around tiny hooves, pointed as a dancer's toes, and
jacked through a groaning pelvis, the heifer stretched
bellowing between posts.

The heifer was down, and Neal watched her strain
and the blue-filmed hooves and nose emerge like a reluctant
diver sliding into air. The heifer was all right, she didn't
need aid or instruction, and when she was back up and
nuzzling the calf, Neal left.

He'd been staying in the bunkhouse with Tom all
winter, an incremental movement away from home and
his boyhood abandoned in the clutter of his room up
under the eaves. As he walked past the kitchen window
he could see his mother at the sink and his father still
sitting at the table, the newspaper spread out before him
but his eyes fixed vacantly on the wall. What was in his
mind? Acres and yields and animal units, remorse for his
anger, or the image of a woman? Neal couldn't imagine.

The bunkhouse was a one-room cabin in the yard behind the house. Neal stepped up on the tie that served as
the porch and opened the door with a lift and a push
from his knee against the resistance he knew it gave in
damp weather. It was dark inside but Tom was there,
lying on his bed smoking. He only smoked when he was
drunk or agitated. Neal sat down on his own bed and
watched Tom's face pull out of darkness and subside
with the slow pulse of his inhalations.

"I haven't seen her for two years," Tom said finally. "The last time was one day out at Point of Rocks when I came back from Oklahoma." He got up and walked to the stove at the end of the room, took the last drag, and opened the lid and threw the cigarette in. He sat down on his bed again and picked up the clock and set the alarm. "I just want to go to sleep," he said, and pulled the covers over his shoulders.

Neal located the boot jack and levered off his wet boots, then lay down and stared into the darkness. He thought again of Myra up on the road in the wind, mouton collar brushing plum cheek, and willed away the knowledge of who she was and got into the car with her instead of Tom and drove away . . .

Neal woke when the alarm rang. He reset it for two hours later as Tom went out—the nightly watch over the expectant heifers. He could see a patch of sky and a few stars and Tom's breath, then the door closed and blinked away the outside. Neal lay awake until Tom came back, bringing the cold in with him.

"There's nothing doing," Tom said.

"Good," said Neal, and turned over, slightly cold and already dreading getting up and going out.

Arlen went to Valerie's that night, not having meant to, knowing that she didn't expect him, but having no other way to quiet the turmoil inside. He was sorry as soon as he pulled into her yard and saw Duane Morton's pickup parked at the fence. He turned around without stopping, knowing that Valerie would hear the truck and know he'd come, and smile secretly behind her beer or against Duane's shoulder, depending on where they'd gotten to in their evening, pleased to deny him.

She wanted him to divorce Florence, and he wanted that too, or thought he did, most of the time. But Florence, tempered by sacrifice and pain and the advice of the Baptist minister, stood firm in her refusal to agree to his terms. She would stay on the ranch, she said, and

run it with Neal, and he was welcome to move on over
to Valerie's and run her place—God knew it needed
some running. Florence knew that Arlen could divorce
her and shame his kids and take up with a cheap bit of
trash like Valerie Pruitt, but he would never bring himself to give up his place.

Arlen drove home and went into the dark house and
lay down on the couch with his boots on. The pains of
Valerie's infidelity, of his inability to subdue her, and
now the reminder of old loss, and of his old self, so
remote and impossible to contemplate because the person he'd become wasn't the person he'd always thought
he'd be, kept him awake in the cold darkness until
dawn.

Chapter Four

Myra sat in her trailer in a park on the banks of
the North Platte River on the outskirts of
Douglas and thought she'd stay a while. There
was something comforting and enclosing about Tom
working for Arlen. Years ago the family had been
close-knit, and they'd had reunions once a year on
Memorial Day or the Fourth of July.

They'd played baseball in the horse pasture on
Memorial Day. She remembered looping fly balls and
splendid catches and the novelty of the men at play.
They all played together, the children and the men, and
sometimes one of the women would be pulled protest-
ing to bat, and if she hit the ball she'd run, giggling and
jiggling, bosom flapping, for first. The men moved in
when the children batted, and pitched slowly, burlesqu-
ing outrageous fumbles until the batter was safely on
first, or all the way around the bases on errors, joyously
proclaiming a home run. But against one another they
were serious and concentrated. Myra remembered playing first base and the power of the men hurtling toward
her, boots thumping, grunting with exertion, the smell
of their sweat and their shade overwhelming her, enclosing her in their aura, and she stood, small and solemn,

in hallowed space, her hand lost in the glove. The sun burned down, the grass curled, and Myra thought of foreign shores, dead soldiers, lilacs, and baseball.

There had been a lot of Dyers in that country back then. There still were, but many had moved away, gone to California. Her family had, back in the sixties, after she'd married Gene and was over by Rock River. They'd raised chickens north of Sacramento, Quinn and Eva Mae, on a ranch Myra never saw, with a palm tree in the yard (oh, symbol of exotic ease), until her father died of emphysema and her mother went back to a sister in North Dakota.

Baseball and firecrackers—and Arlen, kissing her out behind the chicken house, his mouth wet and hard on hers, and him enough bigger to make her believe that he could make her do it, and she'd better not tell. But she knew, and had to admit to herself, that she'd liked it too, and had liked knowing, even thirty years ago, that he could make her let him kiss her but he couldn't make her like him, and that was what he really wanted. She did like him, but she didn't let him know.

A poor-cousin feeling infiltrated her pleasure in the family gatherings. Her family had a place outside of Wheatland—a poor place with a few head of cows and a few hopeless reminders of her father's unversed passion for quarter horses, long-limbed and narrow-chested, whose descendents years later still defined the look of a Dyer cow horse—but a piece of ground of their own. Arlen's folks were in south Laramie then, across from the cement plant, breathing dusty air, selling gas and sundries, and even so they'd thought of themselves as a cut above, with saucers under the cups and ironed pillowcases with tatted edges. Her uncle Ferris believed that Leona and his own backbone raised him above his true nature and the extravagant, sentimental boozing of his brothers.

Myra knew that for all his liking her and wanting to kiss her, she was something vulgar that Arlen didn't want his family to know he wanted. He didn't want to want

her himself and was shamed by their kinship as though
she were struck from a disgraceful rib of his own. He
was the brass ring to her, forever out of reach, and she
assumed a careless air to keep him from knowing how
much it mattered to her.

The reunions fell off with time but the kids saw each
other in the towns and at the dances and rodeos in the
summer. The parents visited and danced on a calm plane
above the turbulence of the children's encounters. The
cousins fought among themselves, taunting and scuffling
between parked cars, locked in combat but united
against the threat of adult intervention. When they
weren't fighting they were tense and watchful, and egged
each other on to smoke sooner, drink more, ride
rougher events. Myra was always there, watching, tag-
ging along, sworn to secrecy on pain of all sorts of imag-
inative torment, comprising their audience and
mediator, medic and second to them all.

When she was thirteen she let Arlen make love to
her on top of a saddle blanket in a horse trailer out behind the chutes at the Guernsey rodeo. It was the Fourth
of July and he was home from college for the summer.

He pulled her by the hand out among the pickups
and trailers behind the chutes as though to show her a
secret, and then, as she had thought he might, he pinned
her against the side of a horse trailer and slid his hand
up under her blouse, kissing her all the while. Then he
was inside her jeans with searching fingers and she
sailed along on the current of his desire. He unbolted
the tailgate and pushed her down on top of a saddle
blanket on the straw.

The pain of his penetration was no more inexplicable
or unexpected to Myra than the sting of an Indian rope
burn administered and endured as a boy's demonstration
of ascendancy, no more outrageous than the tongue
thrusting against her child's teeth while he held her arm
bent up behind her back. More quickly than she had
imagined, it was over, and he knelt above her and buttoned his pants.

"Come on, Myra, let's go," he said. He put on his hat and waited.

Myra had no sense of loss or shame. She sat up in the dim light, dewed by the heat, and grinned at him. Her breasts were low cones rising from the furrowed plain of her rib cage, divided by the flat rift of her sternum, white except for nipples small and flat as pennies. She was happy to be there, but with his passion abated Arlen saw her in another light—now she was an unaccountable kid, his cousin, and he was suffused with remorse. If only she would hurry. He was afraid of discovery and wanted to escape the reproach of her presence, and there she sat in nothing but her jeans and boots, gilded by the angled light, perversely languid. He shook the straw from her blouse and slid it over her arms and buttoned it down the front, enhancing his awareness of her as a child.

As they wound back among the vehicles toward the arena he wasn't holding her hand but striding ahead, eager to lose her. He merged with a group of friends perched on the chutes and from the sanctuary of their company turned and lifted his hand to her.

"See you later," was all he said.

That afternoon she sat in the stands and watched him rope.

Arlen went back to college in the fall without seeing her again and stopped coming home for weekends. Myra heard that he was going to Denver, courting Florence Mayer. She hadn't known how dependent she'd become on the conviction that there'd always be a next time she'd see Arlen and he'd always be in pursuit. Without knowing it she'd disregarded their kinship and linked her future to his, and when he and Florence married her world fell away.

Myra hadn't seen Arlen in years—not since Rock River days when she had run the hotel in blue jeans and a plaid shirt and her hair tied up in a handkerchief to discourage the roughnecks, Tom dragging on her belt loop. It was more a boardinghouse than hotel, a two-story frame in need of paint with its back against the tracks, catering to transients working on the highway or railroad or moving north to the oil fields. By then Arlen had a place on La Bonte Creek near Douglas and he joined the Rock River Grazing Association for summer pasture. He trailed his steers over in the spring and promenaded through town in their wake, knowing that Myra watched from the hotel doorway. He came in later for dinner with his spurs still on to strut before her, scandal and reputation having long since allowed him to shift the guilt for the Guernsey rodeo to her. That was the first time he miscalculated her effect on him. He walked into the hotel with the world by the tail and Myra grinned and said, "Well, hello," and Arlen found a lot of reasons to spend time in Rock River that summer. She poured him coffee and chicken-fried his steaks but he never slept overnight at the hotel. He had no glimmer of insight into the impact his abandonment had had on her.

Myra wondered what he'd think to see her now. She lit a cigarette and watched her reflection flare up in the window.

She wanted to stay. Anything else seemed more than she could bear. She wanted to turn back and tunnel into the comfort and familiarity of the past, to be enfolded back into the circle of the family.

She wondered if Arlen would put her on. Tom had said they were shorthanded, but she'd never worked on a ranch and couldn't remember chores from her childhood beyond feeding the chickens and gathering eggs and submerging her fingers in a pail of milk to encourage a bucket calf to suck.

Driving down the hill that evening and seeing the lights of the house in the surrounding blur of cottonwoods, and the roofs of the barns and sheds, and the corrals spreading toward the creek, she'd felt a lurching desire to be coming home. She would be thirty-six in a

few months. Old, she thought, older than she'd ever
thought of being, and not a whole lot to show for it—
her car and her trailer and the place out by Rock River
that an old man had left to her. She'd had that leased
out ever since and the buildings were just tumble-down
by now. The land never had been much use for anything
except summering. And Tom. Child of her childhood.
But the connection had snapped, stretched to breaking
by separation and neglect. He'd resisted her drifting at
an early age, digging in his heels one fall and refusing to
go. She'd left him in Wheatland with Wells cousins for
school, and after that had only seen him from time to
time in the summers and at Christmas. He was always a
surprise to her—that he was hers, and how much he
wasn't hers at all.

She had flagged traffic on road crews until a dare
from the men boosted her into an apprentice program
that graduated her to heavy equipment. The summer
Tom was sixteen he spent with her near Rawlins, both
of them working on the highway. She had liked that.
They drank beer together after work, sitting on the step
of the trailer, then she grilled antelope steaks for supper
and they listened to the radio and fell into bed before
the light was gone from the sky. It was a peaceful time
for her, with his silent companionship. She'd been sorry
when he was laid off in September and drifted on. He
didn't go back to school, but worked for one outfit or
another, preferring ranch work to the mines or oil fields
despite the low pay.

Myra thought about the years when he was little as
though they had happened in another lifetime. She
recalled the black-and-white border collie that Gene
Wells had had, a good cow dog with its eyes constantly
on Gene's face in anticipation, ready to spring with a
rubbery bound to the back of the pickup, and when he
rode it trotted at his stirrup in his shade. But when Tom
was born the dog completely gave over its responsibilities and would slink around and hide from Gene
when he called, and jump out of the pickup at gates and

trot home to a fretful vigilance at the side of the baby. Gene fumed at this ruination of his best dog but was powerless to break its obsession. Myra was amused and let it inside and fed it under the table.

Tom and the dog spent countless hours in the pickup together, in front of bars and feed stores, in the dark at dances, feeding in the winter and fencing in the summer. More than anywhere else a pickup is home to a dog and a boy in the West. Myra wondered if Tom remembered that dog. Its name had flown her memory.

Chapter Five

The next morning Myra stopped at the house and asked Florence where she could find Arlen. She stood on the porch step, holding the storm door open, the house dog nosing around her, the wind cutting through her jacket, her heart pounding a pulse in her throat.

"Hi, Florence. Long time."

Florence nodded, not giving anything away. "Myra." It might have been yesterday they'd last met.

"Is Arlen around?"

"He's ditching in the oat patch down on the crick," said Florence, her arms a fortress across her bosom.

Myra thought what a hard little hen of a woman Florence had become. "Can I get there in the car?"

Florence thought it over so long Myra decided she wasn't going to answer, and almost turned away, but finally Florence said, "Just go back out to the county road and go right, then take the next right down toward the river. You'll see him."

"Thanks," said Myra and went down the step and through the yard gate and got into her car, Florence's eyes like a gun at her back. She turned in the muddy circle and drove away, rattling over the auto gate.

Arlen saw the car round the contour of the hill and
knew as though he'd lived it before that it was her. He
was at the top end of the field on a yellow Cat straddling the ditch. The car turned into the field and
lurched across last year's pale oat stubble. He kept his
head averted, watching the blade behind him turn up a
neat V of cut earth, feeling her approach like a sun
warming one side of him for minutes before the car
came to rest at a slant a little ahead of the Cat. She got
out and leaned in the angle of the car door. When he
came even with her he shut the machine off and climbed
down.

It was suddenly quiet after the roar of the motor,
only the wind rushing, and like an instant of drowning
the moment dilated and held them suspended.

He stood before her in a characteristic stance, his
fingers in his front pockets, elbows akimbo, rocking on
the heels of his boots. The skin on the back of his neck
and his hands was freckled and red and creased, old
man's skin, and his neck emerged thinly from his collar.
His chapped lips curled back from his white and
prominent teeth in what looked like a smile but was
really part of his squint against the wind and sun.

He flicked Myra with a glance and then his eyes
scanned the field below, and while he fought down the
confusion within he was able to calculate the degree of
dip at the lower end and to rehearse the land planing
process he would use to level the meadow next year.

He brought his eyes back to her face. "Hello, Myra."
She smiled and he felt the old familiar lurch in his chest
that he would have sworn she'd never cause again.
"Tom said you were back."

"I'm back," she agreed, and circled her head with
her arm to pull back her hair. "I quit up at the mine, so
I guess I'm looking for work." She met his eyes again. "I
wondered if you could use me."

He heard the words with a jolt that left him silent
while his mind spun images of the past and future. The
girl's face in his mind's eye confused the image of the

woman before him. The years of thought of her
produced an inappropriate familiarity that he struggled
to conceal, as though their lives were shared in fact as
well as fantasy. A wave of enormous, happy relief rolled
over him at the discovery that he didn't need to pursue
her—she would be there, under his eye, on the place—
and having that assurance, immediately he told himself
that he didn't need her or want her anymore, but only
needed someone for calving and for the trail. "Yes, I
guess I could," he said.

She smiled again and then he leaned too on the open
door of the car, having regained his ascendancy, able to
relax his guard against her, and told her where to park
the trailer down by the creek where they'd had a family
of wetbacks one year and there was a pole and a pump
and a septic tank.

Arlen's impact on her was as it had always been,
heightened by the years. She stopped the car at the
county road and peered into the rearview mirror,
searching her reflection for what she'd seen in his face.
He looked so much as he always had, so like himself,
and yet so aged. Her knowing him had skipped his
prime. He wasn't yet thirty when she last saw him and
now the old man was more visible in him than the boy.

She hadn't predicted that she'd be so overcome, her
awful vulnerability compounded by the flood of old
feeling. She was grateful for the job but afraid to start
thinking about working for him, alongside Tom—work
she'd never done.

When Myra pulled the trailer down the hill, dipping
and bucking and plowing a furrow with the hitch, the
oil pan and holding tank scraping the crown off the
road, Florence stood in the porch behind the screen
with her arms folded and lifted her chin to Myra's wave.
Myra thought of stopping and crept past watching for a
sign of invitation, but none came and she rolled on by

the house and down a faint lane to the cottonwoods by
the creek, flushed with guilt and rejection.

Neal was horseback on the ridge east of the creek when
he saw Myra's car cross the oat field on the other side.
He pulled up and watched and heard the dying rumble
carried on the wind as the Cat shut down. He couldn't
imagine what they said or why she sought Arlen out. If
they'd lifted their eyes in his direction they would have
seen him silhouetted against the clouds. When Arlen
leaned against the car, canting toward her, Neal turned
away and rode on, troubled by a sour curl of jealousy.
But when he came back that afternoon and the wind hit
him as he topped the ridge, cold and raw with melting
snow, and he saw the Cadillac and the trailer below him
in the trees in a bend of the creek, he felt a sudden
springing elation raising his spirits from his boots.
    Clay's hooves slipped in an inch of mud overlaying
the still-frozen ground beneath as they descended the
ridge to the crossing, leaving yards-long tracks behind.
The horse took the crossing reluctantly in disorganized
bounds and scrambled out the other side clattering on
the rocks. Neal was soaked to above the knees and
laughing while Clay bent in a supple curve and danced
sideways against the rein. Myra looked up from where
she crouched leveling the trailer and watched through
the veiling branches, then heels touched ribs and the
horse sprang into a canter and they were gone.
    That night and thereafter the square of light through
the scrim of branches drew Neal's eyes like compass
needles swung to north from all points of the ranch.
What had been an ordinary clump of cottonwoods that
his gaze would sweep past without notice became a
clock of imagined scenes, the progression of lighted windows conjuring images of Myra at the stove with a skil-
let in her hand, eating a solitary meal, yesterday's
Casper Eagle spread under her plate, naked in the
bathroom, the day's clothes kicked behind the door,

brushing her teeth beneath the small frosted pane, and then at the end of the trailer, surely the bedroom, the light remaining past all expectation. What was she doing? Did she fall asleep reading? Did she lie awake smoking? Thinking what? Perhaps she feared the dark and slept like a child with the lights on, her head buried beneath the blankets.

Chapter Six

In the morning Myra milked, the teats like swollen fingers—were they tender? She didn't know how hard to squeeze or pull, bringing too much sentiment to the chore—they were less like nipples than dangling penises—and she looked with apology at the cow. Neal slid in and watched, and she flushed—did he read her thoughts?

"I never milked before."

He knelt beside her, the wool of his jacket a gentle friction against her shoulder. His fingers were long and slender, etched black with grease and oil, and two joints of the little finger of the right hand were missing. Gone how? Myra wondered. Neal caught her glance.

He was eleven, feet flying as he ran in the snow behind the truck, trying to jump on, when the raised stock-rack gate came loose and slammed down like a guillotine onto his hand. He fell skidding to his knees and looked in awe at the gout of blood, then ran for the house. Arlen drove on unaware.

He burst into the kitchen and held up his hand for his mother to see. "Ma!"

"Neal! What's happened?" Florence cried in horror.

"I lost my finger."

"Where? Where did you lose it? Where is it?" she wailed, beginning to move.

"Ma, I lost it. It's gone," crying now, with loss and misunderstanding.

She whipped a clean dish towel from the drawer and wrapped his hand and then was gone through the porch, flinging on a jacket. Neal watched her follow along the trail of blood, and sobbed alone in the kitchen, fragmented and abandoned. She cast around in the snow like a hound, circling and crossing and kneeling to sift the snow with her hands. It seemed like an eternity before she returned, her nose red and her eyes streaming, and bundled him into the car and took him to town.

Neal was forever losing things. He left his jackets at school and could never find his homework papers. Bridles and halters and ropes drifted out of his keeping, and when asked to cast back in his mind to remember, it was like entering a delusive fog.

The first misapprehension that he'd had of her frenzied search never left him. Even later, when he realized that she had hoped to find the severed finger and have it sewn back on, he always had to remind himself that she hadn't run out in vexation because he'd let himself become separated from something he was supposed to take care of. Ever after his missing finger was a reproach and a reminder of his deficiency.

Arlen found the frozen crescent of finger in the back of the truck the next morning and swept it out with the cow manure, and watched as the dog sniffed it doubtfully then picked it up in delicate jaws and trotted off to gnaw it in solitude. Arlen was wrackingly sick beside the truck, and in a small unsung kindness never told Florence.

Neal milked with his face turned away, forehead against
the flank, and the cow let down her milk and it came in
an effortless flow and surrounded them in a warm
vapor. The cats cried and purred insistently and twined
themselves among the cow's legs in an ecstasy of expectation. Myra marveled at their foolish audacity, smoothing their whiskers and flat sides against the fetlocks,
perilously close to the hooves.

Neal turned back to her. "Squeeze from the top and
don't pull so much." She wanted to cry for the failure of
her years to inform the ignorance of her fingers—
instructed by a boy—and was afraid to meet his eyes for
fear she would. He stood up to give her room and
watched as she bent her head against the cow, her hair
falling forward in a tangled curtain, and reached again
for the teats and squeezed as he said. The milk kept
coming, and she smiled up at him.

"It's working," she said.

"You're Myra," he said, and she stood up, letting the
T of the milking stool fall between her feet. She held
out her hand to him. He said, "I'm Neal," her hand in
his, and she felt the stump of his finger against the side
of her palm, and for an instant she lived its loss and her
mind pressed its blunt end against her lips as though to
heal it.

Later she strained the milk into jars on the porch and
took them into the kitchen. Florence stood at the stove
wrapped in faded chenille, turning pancakes.

"Sit down," she said without warmth, but Myra
shook her head. She thought Florence maneuvered for
indebtedness. She stood by the door and waited. It was
warm and the windows above the sink were fogged.
Tom ate swiftly and didn't raise his eyes. Myra
wondered if it shamed him to have her there. She
wished he'd look up. It was hard for her too, to stand
still, an intruder in the kitchen (later she learned it
wasn't her presence that averted eyes and blanketed the
room with silence) and wait to be told what next.

Bonnie sat with a foot in her lap picking at a frosted pink toenail and looked at Myra with impudent eyes, then like a cat stretching she extended her leg, letting the housecoat fall away, and rested her heel on Tom's knee. Tom looked at her sideways and pushed it off, but Bonnie replaced it and laughed. Tom stood up and the foot hit the floor, and Bonnie yelped. This foolishness went past Florence and Arlen as though it wasn't happening, but needled Myra as intended. Tom gave her the tiniest smile as he passed her going out. Saying what? she wondered.

Arlen got up. "Come on," he said, and she followed him to the porch where he layered on enough wool and down for the arctic.

They went out, and through the weeks that followed they fed and fenced and ditched and pulled calves, Myra flat out in a hip-swinging walk to keep up with his headlong rush. They hardly talked. She figured she was supposed to learn by doing or observing, and thought she was equal to anything he showed her except for bull strength, which counted for more than she wanted to admit. In the mornings she climbed into the pickup with him and they crept through the corrals and horse pasture and on down along the creek under an oyster sky with the transmission whining. The business band radio chattered static—Arlen's link to disaster that could jerk him home to a heifer in distress—and the fan circulated dust from the mud-caked floorboards without warmth. The miscellany of past and future catastrophe cluttered the cab—vials of penicillin, syringes, fencing pliers, a balling gun, a spilled box of 30.06 shells. The rifle and shotgun rode behind her head and tire chains beneath her feet. Myra slid out to open gates and close them again after the truck passed through. Sometimes a gate stubbornly resisted, strung so tightly she couldn't lift the loop of wire that held it, and then Arlen waited, the pickup shuddering in a rough idle, long past good sense should have told him she'd never get it. She wrapped her arms around the posts in a desperate embrace,

straining for slack, and swung around to try another
angle, until finally she had to give up and turn helplessly
to Arlen and raise her hands in defeat. Then he got out
without comment, no quip for her to defend against,
just his silent supremacy.

She watched Arlen's eyes sweep the meadows and
hills and saw with his vision the wash of green left by
diminishing drifts, the fur of the willow buds, the
ragged burdock leaves unfurling along the fences. She
watched the shrinking edges of ice along the creek, and
looked at the springing backsides of cows to gauge the
approach of labor. She learned how to load the pickup
with bales so they wouldn't topple off, and how the
truck could drive itself across a meadow in compound
low while she stood on the back and snipped the wires
and flaked the bales to the cows.

She slid in and out of being glad she was there. Arlen
and Tom didn't lose their unexpectedness for her, and
coming upon them daily turned her back in time. She
couldn't place them in the present. It was as though the
forward motion of her life had stopped and she was
slowly revolving in an eddy, divorced from the current.
There were times when it seemed crazy and she thought
she'd let go of her last shreds of dignity—that it wasn't
enough to have spent a lifetime shacking up with dead-
end romance, now she was mooning around in a relapse
of adolescence. But she took pleasure in the tranquillity
of her position on the periphery of the ranch, believing
she could spin out of orbit around it and sail off if she
chose.

Tom lost a calf in the night shortly after she came. In
the morning when she milked she heard Arlen's raised
voice through the wall of the calving shed.

"Well, for Christ's sake, if you couldn't handle it
why didn't you get me, or Neal?"

Neal's voice came in a softer protest, "Dad."

"Well? I'm not saying you should be able to handle
it, but you ought to know if you can't."

She heard only a murmur and couldn't imagine
Tom's reply, though she could picture his face as if he
stood before her, sullen and closed.

Later she saw him fling it—a limp, black-and-white
rag of hide—into the back of the pickup, and she rode
with him to the dump in the draw up behind the house.
Seeing the little body sailing into the back of the truck
and landing with a skidding thud brought back the
plains and the dog they'd had, and she felt a sorrowful
ache for the lost calf and the dog, long since gone, and
for the boy who resided somewhere inside Tom.

"It wasn't me," he said. "Anybody would have lost
it. It just didn't ever get its breath."

They stood in the back of the pickup under a milky
sky, reflected like tapered giants in the dark blue pupil
of the crumpled calf lying at their feet. Myra reached for
Tom. She thought she'd got hold of something that
would lead to his core of hurt and need, but it was like
the tongue of paper streamers pulled from a magician's
mouth that kept coming like unraveling rainbow guts,
then ended and nothing followed, just the last little
paper tail, no heart or blood or gush of tears. His face
was still, his eyes resting in unmarked plains.

"Oh, honey," was all she could think to say.

He threw the calf in the dump on top of cans and
bottles and ancient, unidentifiable machinery, and then
shook the oil drum of ash and charred glass and tin from
the house in over it. It would stiffen and dry and lose its
poignancy as the immediacy of its life departed.

Chapter Seven

There was a late spring blanketing snow, the kind that strands travelers and claims whole crops of lambs and calves. It came on a Saturday, heavy flakes big as quarters falling fast and vertically from a gun-metal sky. By afternoon Arlen decided to bring the pairs in to the corrals. Neal and Tom caught up horses, feeling a holiday exuberance brought on by the novelty of the weather. The horses skittered around with humps in their backs and bogged their heads before trotting out stiff-legged and lively.

By dusk, which fell early, there was a foot of snow and the cows and calves had been moved down to the safety of the ranch and counted, and were eating hay in the horse pasture. Neal and Tom were cold and wet but with undampened spirits. They had been passing a bottle of peppermint schnapps back and forth all afternoon to ward off the chill, and were loaded. They decided to go to town but had to chain up to get up the hill, and when they high centered the pickup by the mailbox they gave up and abandoned the venture. They walked back along their tracks singing "Drop Kick Me Jesus . . . ," and slid down the hill on a flattened box. They walked past the barns and feeding cattle, past the house, and on down the lane.

Myra swung the door back in surprise when they knocked. They stood on the step and blinked in the light like wary colts, good-natured, long-limbed.

"Hi, boys," she said in a flood of confusion and welcome, and stepped back to let them in. They seemed to fill the trailer with the cold air they brought in and their aura of wool and damp and the liniment scent of the schnapps. Myra felt them like a blast in the little room, shoulder to shoulder standing before her, pools of black water spreading on the linoleum as the snow melted from their boots.

"Hi, Ma," said Tom, his face held inward and watchful. Neal nodded in greeting and looked at his boots, then shyly around, avoiding Myra.

Why had they come? What promise had the light of the trailer shining in the cottonwoods held for them as they descended the hill? Myra's heart pounded and she felt her face flushed and unnatural—afraid that like soap bubbles they would vanish. Moments leaped forward like time-lapsed frames and they were sitting at the table with newspapers spread beneath their feet. She had no identity for this. She shook a cigarette from the pack on the table and Tom took one too. He lit hers for her, her head bending forward over the match, then his own, and they looked at each other and smiled. It went through Myra's mind how much Tom looked like Gene Wells around the eyes and cheekbones—eyes that compressed into small crescents above flat cheeks, giving his face the look of a pallid Indian. And she thought how much like Gene he must be in other ways too—less a Dyer than a Wells, a hired man, a drifter, a man who would end his life owning only his pickup and his saddle. How unknowable this boy was to her, and how familiar in his resemblance to his father. She wondered if he drank, if it was a problem for him. And girls? Had his heart broken over some waitress or clerk? Had he made it with a barrel racer down in Oklahoma? Her son, grown to a man, and she had so few memories of him beyond his babyhood, and even the ones from the early days were more like memories of photographs than of shared times. She could see him, small and silent, sitting upright beside the dog in the pickup. She didn't remember him crying, or clinging to her, or needing her. She didn't remember him sick or waking with nightmares. She felt a hopeless, helpless love for him and a guilty acceptance of whoever the being was that he held inside. Whatever he was, she thought, it wasn't of her making, unless you could say that leaving him so much on his own was the making of him.

"Oh, Tom," she said, and he looked up quickly. "Oh, nothing," she said, "It's just been a long time."

With an odd formality that he might use to address a stranger Tom said, "You going to stay around here a while?"

Myra shrugged and looked at Neal, including him in the uncertainty. "I don't know. For a while I guess."

"A.D.'s hard on the help," Neal said and smiled—a question and a warning.

Myra laughed and said, "Oh, I'm doing all right." She was struck, and hated herself for the comparison, by how different the two boys were from one another. She'd known a hundred men like Tom, had served them coffee, worked alongside them, drunk and danced with them, slept with them. It was men like Tom who peopled her life. She didn't think that he hoped for much, and he wasn't likely to be disappointed. But Neal was something else—his father's son. There was a query in his eyes, an assumption that there was an answer that eluded him and he was left bewildered. It was a burden Arlen had carried too, a quest for significance. Neal caught her eyes upon him and she looked away.

Myra fried a chicken and they sat in the brightly lit kitchen and shared what was left of the schnapps as they ate. Afterward Tom piled the dishes in the sink and

pushed the table up against the counter. He turned the
radio up loud and two-stepped his mother around the
patch of linoleum, knees bent and stiffly dipping in time.
Neal sprawled in a chair and let them negotiate around
his legs. His spirits were deflating without the continued
infusion of schnapps. Then Myra pulled him to his feet
and with their arms across each other's shoulders the
three of them kicked and shuffled in a tight wheel until
they were too dizzy to stand.

When Tom and Neal left they thought they might try to
start the snowmobile and go to town on it, or find
Neal's old plastic toboggan stored in the tack room or
buried in the hayloft and slide down the hill some more,
but in the end they did nothing. They walked back to
the bunkhouse, tired and saddened that the promise of
the afternoon had come to nothing more, but without
the spirit to prolong it.

All night in the shallow, fitful, boozy sleep that followed, Neal felt Myra's arm across his back and her
shoulder beneath his hand.

When he was fourteen Neal won the junior calf roping
at the Guernsey rodeo, and in celebration he ordered a
pair of custom calfskin boots with sixteen-inch tops
stitched in hearts and double eagles. He outgrew them
before he wore them out and they had lain in the back
of his closet stuffed with newspapers ever since. He
found them out one night and carried them swinging by
the mule ears down the lane to Myra's. When she
opened the door he held them up like a brace of rabbits
for her inspection, and grinned.

She let him kneel at her feet and her hand rested on
his shoulder for balance as she slid her foot in and
tugged it on. She could have read a warning in this because the table edge would have served just as well. She

felt like Cinderella when they fit, and their exuberance armored her in his youth.

He leaned his elbows on the pink formica table and watched her reflection in the window over the sink as she did three days' accumulation of dishes.

Chapter Eight

A rlen took eight aspirin at once, standing by the pickup and knocking them back with water from a Clorox bottle slung over his shoulder, while Myra watched open-mouthed. They were coming back from Casper with a trailer-load of irrigating pipe and swather parts. He had her drive then, and leaned against the door with his eyes closed, but after another thirty miles he told her to pull over. He vomited in the ditch, then lay down on the gravel beside the pickup with his knees drawn up and his hat over his face.

Myra slid across the seat and cranked the window open to look down at him. "Arlen," she whispered, then more insistently, "Arlen." The only answer was a small dismissing flap of the hand curled in the hollow of his chest. She dug behind the seat and found a pair of torn, insulated coveralls and she climbed out and laid them over him. The arms and legs wrapped him in an insubstantial embrace like a homely succubus. He didn't stir. Myra got back into the cab and listened to the noontime broadcast of Paul Harvey and the Party Line— terrorist bombings, a green broke Appaloosa gelding for sale, and wanted, Haviland Violet cups and saucers.

A county sheriff passed and stopped belatedly half a mile down the road then backed up. He scratched the back of his head while he looked at Arlen, tilting his hat forward over his mirrored dark glasses, then he came back to Myra and grinned. It was her problem, he guessed, and he'd cruise by again in a while.

Arlen got to his feet in the middle of the afternoon and leaned against the door with his head bowed for a long time, then got in like a piece of glass. He looked at Myra with eyes that were all pupil in a blanched face.

"Are you all right?" she asked, leaning toward him. It looked like a plea in his eyes, but perhaps was only pain.

"It's only a headache," he answered, and conjured in Myra's mind handkerchiefs wrung out in ice water and the sachet fragrance of her grandmother's darkened bedroom, all carved mahogany and shades of lilac and mint, at the other end of the house, a whole world removed from dust and manure.

Myra thought she'd drop him at the house, but when they got there he wanted to take the pipe out to the field. They unloaded it into an empty stack yard. He was still moving carefully. The lengths of pipe rolled over each other with insolent clattering that made her cringe for him. When they were done the sun was low and the trees along the creek reached fingers of shadow toward them. Arlen leaned against the fender and took off his hat. His hair lay in a flat, damp tongue against the whiteness of his forehead.

"Dad had them. He'd just drop everything and lay down wherever he was." Arlen looked at her and smiled faintly. "Scared me when I was a kid." Myra wanted to reach for him and pull his head down to kiss away the hurt, and she put the pickup between them to keep from doing it while they watched the light fade from the sky. She resented the pain that, like a mistress, could possess him totally and then release him, spent and limp, without the tiniest flicker left for her.

That night Myra found a bottle of Jim Beam that Vernon had left under the sink, and drank neat shots until
she cried, filled with old longing and confusion. She
didn't think she'd ever seen him defeated, and now
brought to his knees by a tide of blood surging in his
head. The next day she suffered her own headache in
consequence.

It had frozen in the night and Arlen's horse's steps made
hollow-sounding clips as he rode down to the creek on
his way to check the fence line between his place and
the Hughes's. There was a light in Myra's trailer and he
imagined he smelled coffee. He pulled up and con-
templated going in. He watched the square of light but
the window was fogged on the inside and he saw nothing. She'd soon come out to milk. His horse pawed its
impatience and he swung it around and spurred it into
the creek.

Thin, dark ice had formed along the edges in the
night and splintered up like glass. The creek was
down—it would rage soon and swim a horse, but now
the moisture was bound up in the snow in the mountains and Arlen crossed with his boots dry. As he rode
up the ridge on the other side he fancied he heard the
trailer door and in his mind he watched Myra walking
down the lane.

By the time he topped the ridge the eastern sky was
gray and he could see the meadows and pastures below,
white with frost, and the dark snakes of the creeks. Most
of what he saw was his, wrestled to him chunk by
chunk, the hard way, with the lenders looking over his
shoulder. Seeing so much of it spreading out before him
made him suddenly tired—tired out by spent effort and
effort yet to come. Husbandry wasn't enough except for
those who came into their land. He had to be lawyer
and conniver, putting on his worsted pants and sitting
for hours in the bank with heartless fools who spoke
only numbers. It had started as a game he'd liked to

play. He was scornful of small outfits too timid to ex-
pand, but now, with a million dollars owing and cattle
prices down, the bankers told him what to do and he
had to scramble to stall them off. All this built from
nothing.

He had started on a leased place north of town, two
tanks and no creek at all, and the family in a cleaned-out
chicken house. He'd started his herd there and after a
few years he'd had enough to borrow against to buy the
Wagonhound place.

It was a small place but it had the creek and some
good meadowland, and he bought into the grazing association then for pasture. Florence was happy. The kids
were little and she liked the house down in the cottonwoods and box elders out of the wind. Then the flood
came, wiping them out one spring afternoon.

Arlen had spent the morning on horseback in the
rain trying to push the cows up out of the meadows, but
they wanted to shelter from the storm in the brush and
trees along the creek and they drifted back. His horse
was lathered and stumbling when he swam it home, and
it trotted away into oblivion under Arlen's high-cantled
saddle tooled in an all-over basket-weave, head held
sideways to avoid the dragging rein.

Florence had watched the creek rise all morning and
by afternoon swollen bodies of cows were churning by
with the cottonwood debris. When Arlen came in
soaked and shaking, they headed on foot for higher
ground up behind the house. Arlen carried Bonnie while
Florence dragged Neal by the hand, and they only just
made it in time, clawing their way upward in the greasy,
red mud. They sat on a tilted shelf of rimrock in the rain
and watched a wall of water rush through the house. It
left the two side walls standing supporting the roof and
swept through between, taking everything.

Arlen mourned on the hillside that afternoon, but the
next day he was out again on a borrowed horse, assess-
ing the damage, scouring the hills for the few remaining
cows, saving what he could.

He stopped going to town, unable to face the sympathy and satisfaction he met in the feed store or the
auto parts store, as people saw in him a confirmation of
the prudence of their own limited aspirations. He
refused to be defeated and denied Florence her grief. He
left her with a friend in town where she dressed herself
and the children in the humiliation of charity and
donated castoffs. Arlen slept in his pickup and ate with
the neighbors. He recognized only his own losses; what
were baby pictures and a great-grandmother's quilting
against the lives of cattle and horses and the years of his
invested labor?

The cattle lay in great balloons, knitted together with
fence wire and tree limbs along the creek bottom, and
they spoke to him in the sighing of intestinal gas and the
buzzing of iridescent blankets of flies. Months later he
found his horse beached halfway up a sidehill a mile
below the house, its sun-cured hide draped across naked
bones like a child's rainy day tent of blankets and chairs,
and he cut the nickel silver conchos from the saddle
strings.

They had cut cordwood on the Wagonhound for
years and still the cottonwood ghosts lay like jackstraws
along the creek bed. From where he rode, Arlen could
look down and see the new trees, box elder and cottonwood and willow, grown up through the tangle. Part of
himself had been swept away that day too, and he sometimes fancied he'd come upon it again someday along
the creek and reunite with his hopefulness and the part
of himself that could look forward, melding selves, and
go on into the future complete. He had hoped to build
something enduring to pass through generations but the
flood had washed him clean of the belief that it was pos-
sible. He went on, building and acquiring, carving
meadows out of hillsides and pasture out of prairie, but
he thought of it as a delicate superstructure poised on
his shoulders, ready to tumble back into component
parts with his smallest misstep. He held the total
knowledge of his ranches in his mind like a map he

could look inward upon and see the silver threads of irrigating water, the patches of turned earth, the cattle
and fences, and the ants of Neal and Tom and Myra that
he moved like players on a board.

Arlen came to the common fence line high on the
ridge across the Wagonhound. Some of the fence posts
were juniper stumps as thick as a man, and there were
stretches of wire ferocious as sharks' teeth that were
part of the original drift fence that the Hughes'
grandfather had put in to keep his cattle this side of the
Rockies. It was a canker eating at Arlen's neighborliness
that the land adjoining him was Hughes land and had
been since ownership began. The first Hughes had had it
all to pick from and had taken the best in a great V between the La Prele and Wagonhound with the wide end
along the Platte. It had succeeded from Hughes through
his son and now was split three ways between Gilbert,
George, and Gary. Registered herds grazed belly deep in
fields Arlen would have hayed. Gilbert was a state
senator, a rancher in name only who papered one wall
of his living room with U.S. Geological Survey
topographical maps with the Hughes holdings outlined.
He had a racquetball court built in his basement. George
was a veterinarian. Only Gary ran his own third, with an
annual parade of wetback labor under him.

Arlen couldn't think of the Hugheses without two
things springing up in his mind. One was what lucky
bastards those three were, and if he stood in their boots
with meadows and creeks and pastures, and with forest
service adjoining, and all handed down free and clear,
he'd have made more of it than any one of them. The
other was a welling, choking, suffusing anger at Neal because for four years, all the while Neal was in high
school, Arlen had thought that in a logical and deserved
destiny he would merge with the Hugheses. That it
wasn't turning out that way rested on Neal's head. Julie
Hughes had worn Neal's tape-wrapped ring as a har-
binger to diamonds until she went to college. Arlen
didn't know what Neal had done to lose her, but she

was irretrievably gone, studying veterinary medicine in South Dakota, and engaged to her father's small-animal associate.

Neal had come into the kitchen one night walking carefully and leaned up against the counter, a wide leather belt wrapped around his hand, the silver buckle across his knuckles like a shield. "You're drunk," Florence said, disgusted.

Neal nodded and grinned foolishly. "Me and Julie broke up," he said.

Arlen got to his feet. The belt made sense now. Julie had worn it as a trophy or a brand, the tongue doubled back over itself to keep the excess from flapping and the "Neal" tooled among the rosettes riding around over her kidney she was so slim. "You asshole. What did you do?" Neal's head dropped and wagged dumbly from side to side. Arlen grabbed him by his shirt front and shook him. "What did you do?"

Neal looked up. His eyes swam. The belt unwound from his hand and dropped to the floor. "She doesn't love me, Dad," he said, an admission of failure and loss.

Here was the glue that was bonding Arlen to the past and the future he yearned for dissolving with Neal's tears. He picked up the belt and snaked it out across Neal's chest. "You shit, of course she doesn't love you. Look at you." Neal turned and bent against the counter and his father whaled at his back and shoulders. Florence clung to Arlen's arm. He shook her off but abandoned Neal and cracked the belt against the counter and the table, swirling in an operatic tantrum around the room, swinging at the door jams and chair backs, holding the buckle in both hands, until he spun Neal around again. "How could you lose her? What did you do?"

Neal covered his eyes with his hand and drew in a shuddering breath. "I don't know, Dad. I didn't mean to. I love her." Arlen shoved him away and Neal stumbled against the door to the porch, and went out to lie all night on his back in a saltbox under a windmill up by the county road, lacerated by self-pity and self-loathing. He saw himself with his father's eyes—thin, gooney boy, drunk, dissipating his mourning with tears and alcohol.

That was four years before. Neal wore the belt again himself, its edges deeply frayed.

Arlen thought of Julie as a perfect shining fish with the hook in her lip, played close but lost in Neal's eagerness, flashing away glinting in the sun, to mock them from her domain.

Arlen patched fence along the high ridge all day among sagebrush laced with crusted snow like shelves of sugar, and thought about the first Hugheses who'd come out in the nineties and strung the wire and sunk the posts, and he cursed his own grandfather who'd ground to a halt in Minnesota.

Chapter Nine

Myra stood before the mirror and hung her jaw open and gazed into the reflected cavern at the little brown hole in her bicuspid where the filling had been. It hurt as the air sucked over it. Neal had said chew would help. She wondered. She'd like to pack it with something until she got to the dentist. She closed her mouth and looked at her face. She thought aging wasn't a gradual process, it befell her suddenly, stepwise. Just when she grew accustomed to one line or puff and thought she knew what she looked like, it happened again. She was never caught up and was always sorrowing for the lost face.

She smeared on a thick layer of Vaseline and rubbed it in. Fine, pale lines rayed out from the corners of her eyes—delicate, white spiders in her tan, sheltered from the sun by her squint.

The next day she went to Casper and spent an hour with her head cradled in the dentist's firm, impersonal grip, her eyes on Neal's boots neatly crossed at the end of the chair, waiting for it to be over. Afterward she bought an extravagant pair of doeskin gloves to forestall the effects of work and weather on her hands, and decided on a drink.

She sat with her back to the bar drinking Coors with half her mouth while the other side tingled back to life. Behind her she was overhearing a tale of a semi-truck wreck, and with slowly dawning recognition she realized that the voice belonged to Lloyd Wells and the driver he was talking about was Gene. She swung around and listened unabashedly then, and watched as Lloyd's attention was engaged by her interest and it came over him who she was. He was drunk and he fell silent looking at her. He slid from his seat at the bar and came to her table and reached for her hand with both of his.

"Myra," he said, not a greeting but a declaration, as though he'd chased around in his mind for a summation of something and that was it. His little finger curled frozen into his palm from an old, bad dally, and she felt it like a small, obscene hard-on as he held her hand. He took his time marshaling himself to retell the story. His bridgework was in his cigarette pocket and his tongue flickered in the gap.

"Gene always set a lot of store by you," he said, and with that she knew the end of it. The rest of the story, when she got it, wasn't much. Gene had failed to make a corner trucking rodeo stock through the Wheatland canyon. Lloyd told her more than she wanted to know about what happened to the stock when the trailer rolled, and what the rodeo people and insurance company had to say, and more, too, than she wanted to know about the injuries that killed her husband. It was a surprise to her how affected she was, and she had to fight down an impulse to get drunk and eulogize him with Lloyd. She thought of Gene driving drunk and fast through the night and of his last moments when he must have known that the truck wouldn't hold the curve. Now that the possibility had departed forever, Myra perversely thought she'd like to see Gene again. His brother, this Lloyd before her, stiffened by age and injuries, an old rodeo buckle a proud oval of championship at his waist, at home with his drunkenness, a hopeful, goatish leer in his eyes as he looked at her, brought Gene flooding back.

Gene had had a crow's wing of hair across his forehead and a knee that wouldn't unbend, and when he'd started coming out to the ranch, drinking beer and pitching horseshoes with her father and talking bloodlines, she had let him know she liked him. He was thirty, more than twice her age, and it didn't take good sense to see he was heading nowhere, but Myra was still reeling from Arlen's marriage and she let herself be courted. He sat beside her on the porch and let his hand slide down her thin, brown arm to her hand and his man's thumb scraped at her chipped pink polish. He was awed by what she would allow, faint and short of breath. Complicity smiled at him from the corners of her eyes. He draped his arm heavily across her shoulders and twisted a curl of dusty hair around his finger, furtiveness giving way to familiarity. He couldn't believe his luck when she said yes. She was fourteen when they married—a scandal. People said that Quinn Dyer had always been careless with his things. Quinn hadn't liked it, and had tried to talk her out of it, and Eva Mae had wept, but Myra had made up her mind. She packed her bag one Friday night and went off with Gene. She walked through the front room and said, " 'Bye, Ma. 'Bye, Dad," and left them frozen in astonishment.

Myra and Gene found a woozy justice of the peace in Baggs, too shortsighted to focus beyond the proffered fifth of Ten High, and honeymooned in a motel in Rawlins.

Gene took her home to the headquarters of the Grazing Association, a treeless scatter of buildings on the plains huddled in the angle of a flattened tin windbreak, loose corners flapping and screaming, and planted Tom before Quinn and Eva Mae were organized enough to object. Gene ran a few cows of his own and looked after the fences and windmills. The summers were busy with a lot of stock on the plains but they didn't winter anything except their own few head. Gene started drinking heavily in the winter. He sat in the bar in Rock River through the afternoons and came home at night raging against Myra. She was fifteen and Tom was a baby, keeping her home, erasing her childhood. She was an oddity in town when she went in for groceries, like the sawyers' wives, woods people who drifted up from Texas to cut fence posts, defensive and inarticulate, cut off from the comforts of convention. The women she met in the store or on the street looked at her furtively out of the sides of their eyes, their own babies riding their hips with confidence and honor.

Gene left her in the pickup with the motor running while he sat in the bar for a quick one, until she had to come to the door and call for him, Tom fretting in her arms. Heads swiveled down the line of the bar and someone said, "Hey, Gene, here's your kids," and they called out to her, saying, "Darling," and "Honey," and teasing her to come in until she did, for spite, and sat down a few stools away from Gene and asked for rum and Coke, silencing them all. Gene spun off his stool and hustled her home. She was such a prize to him, and he had thought that marrying her would make her his, but he discovered he couldn't possess her. Her warmth and smile and the light in her eyes were as stupifyingly desirable and impersonal and remote as ever.

At home Myra sipped the whiskey she kept to rub on Tom's teething gums to ease the edges of the dragging hours, and she floated through the months.

Gene started knocking her around. He could affect her that way, could make her cry, but he couldn't make her turn to him. She held herself more and more away from him. He came home, bucking through drifts of blown snow, the light in the kitchen a false promise visible for miles and miles, and she'd be there by the stove, her feet in the woodbox, reading a western novel while Tom sat on the floor and picked Cheerios up off the linoleum.

It tore Gene up, wanting to be everything to her and feeling like nothing at all. He lost the Grazing Association through drink and neglect, and Myra took Tom and moved over to a neighboring ranch with a man old enough to be her grandfather. She had lived with Gene just under three years.

It suited her to be with the old man. She liked him and she was the world to him. She stayed a few years, until he got sick and his people came and got him and took him to Laramie to die.

Gene had been gone from Myra's life for so long, except in memory, his death made no real difference. He'd go on with as much substance as ever in her thoughts. But he wouldn't be piling up memories for anyone else anymore. She supposed he would have grayed as Lloyd had done. She was older now than he was in her memory.

But when she left the bar that night it wasn't Gene or Lloyd she was thinking of, but Tom. The accident was old news. It had happened back in the fall and Lloyd told her that Tom had come over to Wheatland for the funeral from Arlington where he was working. He'd said "Tommy," a diminutive she had never used, with affectionate familiarity. She hadn't known, had never thought, that Tom had gone on having any relationship with his father. She'd let Gene out of her life like a cat into the night, and had never figured that he couldn't slip as easily from Tom's. She wasn't sorry or jealous, but glad that there was a web of more than just her supporting him in life, but even so it made fiction of her past assumptions. He had kept silent about his Wells relations and it made him less a Dyer than ever in her mind. She wondered if he'd taken it hard. Like a fox he'd never let it show.

Chapter Ten

Neal lay down on the seat of his pickup. He could sleep for fifteen minutes in the meadow before he caught the calf. The night before he had lain awake in the bunkhouse until the sky lightened, but now he felt he could sleep for a year. His eyes wandered around. A chain of linked pop tops that must stretch a quarter of a mile looped around the rifle rack, souvenirs from a river of beer. He thought he should get that out of there—if he were to see a coyote he'd never get his gun untangled in time to shoot. It had been four years since he graduated and it hadn't meant anything anyway, so why was the tassel from his mortarboard still hanging from his mirror? Julie's had hung there too for a while—blue-and-white hula skirts shimmying together. He didn't miss her anymore, or even think about her much. It didn't have any more reality than the memory of a dream.

He was floating. He had to keep his thoughts away from what lay ahead. He could get through the days, one by one, hour by hour, but he couldn't let himself think of the future, days stacked up against one another, thin and meaningless as cards in a deck. He slept.

When he woke the sky was graying and he knew it
had been more than fifteen minutes and that the afternoon had slid by. The scouring calf was down, lying flat
and frail on its side. It had little strength to resist and he
tackled it without a rope and laid it panting in the pickup. He'd doctor it at the barn and keep it in for a few
days if it lived. The cow trotted behind the truck, bray-
ing her muddled concern.

Later, rather than chase sleep through the night, he
went to town and sat by himself in the Plains for a
couple of hours, drinking beer like an old-timer. He
didn't feel drunk when he left but he took the turn by
the Town Pump a little wide and fishtailed in recovery.
Maybe it looked worse than it felt because a cop stopped
him and took him in on a DWI.

They let Neal make a phone call and he woke
Florence up. He told her there was no way to post bond
until Monday and he'd spend the weekend playing cards
with old man Hughes who'd been picked up for for-
nicating with the checker from Duke's supermarket
under his four-wheel drive out in front of the La Bonte
Hotel. Neal cracked himself up telling her about it and
the cop took the phone away.

Later that night Neal heard his father carrying on
with the desk sergeant. It surprised him that Arlen had
come to town, but he didn't delude himself about the
reasons. It had probably looked like the thing to do, and
now Arlen was pissed off because someone else was
making the rules. Neal knew that Arlen wouldn't want
to spring him, but he'd want to be able to and then not
do it. After a while Arlen's voice was joined by Gary
Hughes's milder rumble—come to bail his daddy out,
only to discover, as Arlen had, that it would have to
wait. The voices calmed and there was some laughter,
then Gary shouted back, "See you Monday, you old
goat!" but Mr. Hughes was dead to the world, curled in
satiety with his hands clasped between his thighs.

Tom dosed the calf but it died anyway on Sunday
afternoon. Neal had to suppress the nagging, useless

guilt that if he'd doctored it right away and hadn't slept maybe it would have lived, and he would have stayed home.

Arlen's short temper and black moods and comings and goings gradually took on a pattern for Myra and she figured out that he was seeing someone. It first came to her on a Thursday evening as she watched him spin up the hill in a hurry on the heels of Florence, who was going in to Weight Watchers. Myra felt as though she'd swallowed a rock, and she had to sit down where she was in the dust beside the barn as her mind flipped back. She knew it with an illogical certainty. But who? Her impulse was to fly up the hill on his tail and follow him until she found out. Then what? Scratch her eyes out? Arlen had lain in the back of her mind like a remittent destiny for so long she had felt composed and patient, in no hurry to alter her relationship with him, but she'd been turning over the possibilities since she'd come, never thinking there might be another snake in the garden to tempt him. She felt a sudden surge of fellowship with Florence—he betrayed them both. No wonder Florence looked at her out of ironical eyes.

He'd had on a white shirt, and his gray beaver hat that still had some shape to it. Cleaned up he looked younger, with an antique elegance, his reddish beard, untrimmed all winter, grazing his chest. He was eating Florence's dust—she'd have him in the rearview mirror—so he wasn't even pretending to keep it from her.

Myra got up and walked on to the house with the milk. As she strained it on the porch she could see through the kitchen to the dark living room where the flickering light from the television illuminated boots and blue-jeaned legs. She couldn't see the rest of the boys. Neal and Bonnie and Tom had gone in together on a satellite dish last winter. They were probably watching blue movies beamed in from space. It made Myra sick and sad to think of them sprawled there, dull and inert.

There wasn't much that they got up to that cast her down, but this did.

She went into the kitchen and rearranged things in the refrigerator so she could fit the milk. She wished they'd turn the television off and emerge and talk to her. She would ask where Arlen had gone and read who knew what on their faces. In their presence she would feel alive again with potential.

She went out without talking to them but she slammed the kitchen door so they'd be sure to know she'd been there.

Myra went home and dug through her closet for a flannel dress of gathered tiers she'd worn once to a street dance after a rodeo, her waist cinched by a concho belt. She put it on and looked in the mirror, then crumpled on the bed and cried into the skirt— tears for the vanished sweetness that had clothed her in the hopefulness of dresses—sweetness that now stood Arlen before his mirror brushing his hat and snapping into a pressed shirt for someone else. Myra wished she were the peahen he fanned his tail for.

She hung the dress back in the end of the closet, a prudent corner of her mind counseling thrift—she would recover and might dance in the street again. She wondered what Arlen could have read in her looks, and flushed to think that her desire might have betrayed itself in dilated pupils or the list of her body toward him. She hadn't even the dignity of youth to retreat into.

She pulled on her blue jeans again, like a familiar skin, and a sweatshirt, and sat in the kitchen with her feet on the table and drank Vernon's warm Jim Beam in a toast to her unknown rival, and laid down her banners of hope and expectation.

Chapter Eleven

Saturday Myra went to town. She came in from
irrigating and threw her clothes in a pile on the
bathroom floor, stood in the shower for twenty
minutes (oh, luxury of hot water), then dried her hair
and put on weekend listick, and loaded the laundry
into the trunk of the car. It was cloudy and warm, with
a surprising south wind turning the new cottonwood
leaves belly up in the trees.

Arlen flagged her at the house, standing hatless in
the door and shouting as she passed. His irrigating boots
were draining upside down by the porch, and she followed the footprints his wet socks made on the worn
wood into the kitchen. He wanted her to pick up a fitting for the irrigation pump on the Wagonhound place.
That's where they'd been all morning, Arlen and the
boys, wet to their waists in the frigid runoff, fussing
with the submersible pump. He shook in spasms of chill
and his hands were blanched beneath the freckles—all
his blood retreating inward to his vitals. He showed
Myra the fitting and told her where to get its replacement. She had an urge to take his poor hands in her
own and to breathe on them, or to cup them, one on
either side of her breasts, and clamp them there in her

armpits to warm them; but the impulse to kindness aroused her again to betrayal and she hardened her heart. Let him freeze, she thought, it was stubbornness that made him suffer, and perversity, for he'd only ask of the boys what he expected of himself, and he wished for their suffering more than for his own comfort.

"You're not going to want this before tomorrow, are you?" asked Myra. She didn't want to hurry back out with half-dry laundry and cut short whatever possibilities rose up in town. As soon as she said it she could tell that he did want it, but he wouldn't ask on her half day off. If he wants it that badly, Myra thought, Florence can go. He was looking at her and Myra thought she read surprise in his eyes. He knew she had suddenly cooled and he'd be wondering why, mentally clicking back to recall his mistake.

"No, tomorrow's okay," he said.

Florence gave her a tight, little smile. "You want me to pick anything up for you?" Myra asked her.

"No thanks," said Florence.

Myra drove into town. The wind was chasing tumbleweeds and bits of paper across the road, and the river gave back the gray of the sky. She dropped the clothes in the damp, harvest gold rows of the laundromat, then went to Safeway and trailed through the aisles with half the county. As she crossed the parking lot, wrestling her basket of groceries against the wind and incline, she lost track of where she was for a moment—all the Saturdays stretching backward and forward, the Safeways, homogenizing the countryside—it could as easily be Rawlins or Laramie and she was spacing her life out between trips to the supermarket. She wanted a beer to put down the panic. She pulled across the street to the Alibi and bought a case of Coors in the package store, then eased into the afternoon gloom of the lounge, where she drank two beers in the company of a couple of old guys with wives at Safeway.

She felt a little better, and picked up the pump part, glad she had remembered, then drove back to the laundromat and put the clothes in the dryer. She went to the Silver Dollar then, and drank sweet white wine until she calculated the clothes would be dry.

The sky was darker and the wind blowing harder than ever when she carried the clothes basket out of the laundromat, and she was cheered by a little early neon down the street. She started for home but changed her mind and made a U-turn by the fairgrounds and drove back through town to the Roundup. The idea of going home to the trailer in the dusk and fixing herself something to eat and then falling into bed early and alone was too much to bear. She was glad that Arlen wasn't waiting for the pump fitting. She pictured for a moment his anger if he was, he'd be pacing and coiling tighter and tighter inside. Well, anyway, she'd told him she wouldn't be hurrying on that account.

She went into the bar and ordered a beer. She knew that heads turned. She let her eyes run quickly over the faces reflected in the mirror behind the bar—speculative Saturday night faces. She took her time drinking the beer, then ordered another and carried it into the restaurant and sat alone by the window and ate a rib-eye steak, cooked rare—cooked by someone else.

She knew it wasn't a good idea, but after she ate she went back into the bar. This time when she looked down the line of faces she noticed who was looking back. By the time the band started playing an unemployed oil field mechanic on his way south was sitting beside her buying her beer. They danced and she let him hold her close and nudge his knee between her legs. He had his thumb up between her shoulder blades to guide her and her arm straight at the elbow and angled off behind her, and they traveled around the floor in spins and glides. The visor of his cap grazed her ear. He knew what he wanted, and if she wasn't going to wake up in the morning in his camper she was going to have to start fending him off.

She went to the bathroom and sat on the toilet and tried to think. She wondered where Arlen was tonight.

Warming up in a hot bath, rosy below the water line?
Myra thought she'd like to warm him up, and could do
it too, but he was more than likely rolling in someone
else's arms tonight, warming his blood in tangled sheets.
She held her head and tried to imagine how she'd feel in
the morning, waking up parked in a line of dieseling
semis with a cotton mouth and bags under her eyes and
no very clear recollection of the time they'd had, trying
to look this guy, whose name she already couldn't
remember, in the eye. He'd be wanting to pull out early
to make Oklahoma and she'd smile and climb into her
clothes and pretend it didn't matter, and with downcast
eyes she'd buy coffee-to-go in the Roundup to drink on
her way home. Would Arlen be there to see her pull past
at daybreak? Would she spark a flame of jealousy in
him? Myra got up and stood in front of the mirror. She
looked ghastly in the fluorescent light.

      She left through the restaurant without saying good-
bye and got in her car and headed for home.

She had a flat on the on-ramp. It took her a minute to
identify the sudden flap and rumble. She pulled onto the
shoulder and stopped and got out. She sat on the back
bumper with her head in her hands and laughed. She
should have stayed. She didn't even know if her spare
was any good. The wind was just off body temperature,
like a live thing preening itself against her, nosing up
under her shirt, circling her ribs and fluttering against
her. She lay back on the trunk and closed her eyes and
tried to ride out the boozy spin. A semi roared by on the
highway above her, buffeting her with its wake of wind
and peppering her with blown dust. She might have
slept for she couldn't have said how long it was before
she was pinned in the lights of an approaching vehicle.
She sat up and turned her head, waiting for the glare to
pass, but the pickup pulled in behind her, its outside
tires crunching on the gravel of the shoulder. The engine died and the lights went out but their brightness

remained on her retinas, so it was from a nimbus of dancing sun dogs that Neal emerged. Myra blinked.

"Hi," she said.

"Hi," he replied, grinning.

She was overcome with gratitude for his presence—he assured her reaching home—but to her horror she felt tears start up in her eyes. "Oh, shit. I had too much to drink in town, and now I've got a flat," she said, and turned away, trying to blink back the tears. Neal watched her.

"Well, hell, it's nothing to cry about," he said.

"No," she said, "I'm not, it's your lights. They made my eyes water."

"Do you have a spare?" he asked.

Myra stood up and moved aside. Neal lifted the trunk and shifted the laundry basket and bags of groceries around until he could pull out the spare tire. Myra relinquished the task to him and sat down on the side of the road, her arms around her knees. Behind her Neal searched around in the trunk for the jack. The sounds of his activity—setting the jack when he found it, the ratcheting as he raised the car, the little clangors and thuds of the tire iron against the resisting nuts, the spin as they loosened, and the plunks and rolling diminuendos as the nuts spun in the hubcap—reached her with the comfort of familiar noises from another room penetrating a sleeper's consciousness. She drifted. Finally she heard the trunk close and Neal's boots passing behind her in the gravel, and his pickup door opening. She wondered if he was leaving, but when she looked up he was standing beside her again, offering a beer.

"God, that's the last thing I need," she said, but she took it. Neal sat down beside her. They drank their beers without talking, staring through the mesh of the easement fence to the lights of town. Myra felt the heat of his arm next to hers, and the hairs of his forearm grazing her skin in the whisper of a caress. She watched the distant jerky descent of the Roundup's pink neon lariat and was glad again she hadn't stayed.

"I think I'll go on home," Myra said after a while, and smiled at him. "I'm glad you came along." Neal got up and helped her to her feet, her elbow sharp and heavy with unsteadiness in his hand.

"I'll follow you home," he said as he closed her door, and his lights, on low beam a considerate distance behind her, kept her within the circle of his concern all the way home. She was glad the heavy car held the road pretty well on its own—he wouldn't be alerted by her weaving to how far gone her judgment was.

Chapter Twelve

S pring progressed. Stubborn drifts melted in the
lees, leaving behind startling patches of emerald,
and a celadon wash swept over the hills. Myra
couldn't shake off the pain of relinquishing Arlen a
second time; it lay within her, a dimension of her
interior that her mind and heart could palpate, that
dwindled with time but could unexpectedly swell at
sight of him.

She plowed mile after mile of furrows through the
bottom land, and disced and harrowed and seeded. The
effluvium of the turned earth carried her back to her
childhood and her mother's garden. She remembered
walking barefoot behind as her mother severed the
heads of cabbages, and the squash vines twining from
hills of dung. The garden was a steamy island fenced
away from the droughty corrals and pastures, a drip
hose like a sweating snake stretched among the
vegetables.

Her father was full of booze and resentments and im-
practical schemes. He took the milk cow calf to the sale
barn one night and came home with a rangy, speckled
stallion from Colorado like a ticket in the Irish
sweepstakes. Despite its unlikely appearance the horse

could sprint, and Quinn trucked it around four states in
the back of his pickup, to fairs and rodeos, racing it and
putting it to stud. It never made him much money but
earned him, in his own estimation, the stature of a
horseman, canny and able to see through faults to heart.
The descendants of this long shot could still be seen in
Arlen's Easter and John's Babe, and countless others
through the years in the Dyer's corrals with high withers
and narrow shoulders and both front legs coming out of
the same hole. In Myra's memory her father was a ban-
tam in faded blue jeans belted low, preferring talk to
work and society to solitude.

She thought she would like to see their place west of
Wheatland again. They had scrabbled by in a kind of
hard rock existence, doing without indoor plumbing
long after most of their neighbors had running water in
their kitchens and tacked-on, lean-to bathrooms with
flush toilets, leaving the outhouses to tilt in the wind in
the corners of the yards, and grass to grow up in the
trodden troughs between back door and privy. They had
hauled their drinking water from town because the rusty
red alkaline hill water in their well was only fit for
stock. The rooster tail of dust kicked up by a car or
truck on the county road was visible for miles, and Myra
remembered the way her mother would watch its
progress, tension growing at the approach of company,
her hands smoothing her apron and the nervous quick
check in the mirror over the sink, furtive in case of disappointment. They seldom had a visitor. The dust cloud
usually turned away on someone else's ranch road or
traveled beyond the hill that their road skirted. If the
dust disappeared behind the hill there were moments of
suspense before it reappeared winding further into the
hills, or suddenly closer and surely coming to them.
Then quickly, leaning toward the mirror, in two curving
strokes, Eva Mae applied a bow of lipstick and rolled the
color onto her lower lip, hurrying now so as to have
time for bogus nonchalance. Myra and Stanley hung like
monkeys over the sofa back in the front room, guessing

and contradicting each other about the identity of the
visitor.

Neither her mother nor father inspired much confidence or respect, and Myra weaned herself early of any
need of them. She had communicated little with them
after they had gone to California, and she hadn't missed
them since they had died. She wondered if they'd been
happy. They were like the furniture of her childhood,
taken for granted and ignored and now hard to conjure
back in memory except for a few black-and-white scenes
flickering across her mind, then trailing off.

Her brother was gone too—Stanley. Shot dead one
night when he was twenty-four on a deserted stretch of
county road outside Thermopolis, found beside his pickup with his pants down around his knees, and it was a
horror to Myra to think of what had come first, the
shotgun blast to the chest or the practiced castration,
work of some trailer house riff-raff whose wife Stanley
was balling. She turned her mind from him—there were
probably more than a few who thought he'd had it coming.

She cheered the earth as it brought up the faint green
of young oats and alfalfa in the fields she'd plowed. She
irrigated, and learned to turn the water out across the
fields in a sheet, moving and rebuilding the dams of
plastic and wood and field stones in the ditches.

One Saturday she turned over a patch of ground near
her trailer by hand and put in cabbages of her own, and
lettuce and carrots and pole beans in a tepee. In the evening when she was nearly done, Tom came and
hunkered with his back against a tree watching her in
silence. Myra watched him watching her and when the
last peppers and tomatoes were in and under hats of
folded newspaper she went and sat down beside him.
He grinned at her and she couldn't fathom the meaning
in his look. She hadn't gardened much when he was a
boy out on the plains. The wind flattened everything

and sucked the earth dry. Did he smile to see her now scratching in the earth like an old hen? She was sweating in Vernon's old shirt. He gave her a pull on his beer and she lit a cigarette.

"I'll cook you supper," she said.

Tom straightened up against the tree. "Naw," he said, "I'm going to town."

She had spoiled the moment by trying to insure more, and now he was going, but her pleasure in her garden was undiminished and she went on sitting there long after he walked away.

Chapter Thirteen

Neal was hooking the six-horse trailer to his pickup when Myra walked past. He backed under the gooseneck, leaning out his open door to guide himself. Myra stopped and watched him as he got out and cranked the weight of the trailer down onto the bed of the truck. He looked at her. "You want to go to Glendo?" he asked.

"What for?" asked Myra.

Neal moved quickly and in a moment he was back in the pickup, revving the engine in surges, rocking the truck and puffing clouds of dust up from beneath the tail pipe—all those horses in trembling containment. "Come on, go with me. I might need some help," he said.

He made her want to go, smiling at her from the visor shadow of his cap, but she shook her head, her hands deep in her pockets, rocking on her heels, turning down his invitation to hooky. Neal leaned across the seat and swung open the passenger-side door and jerked his chin at her in good-natured command. "Get in," he said, sending a thrill of surprise and pleasure through her to be asked again. Her eyes shifted away as she let herself consider what had only a moment before been

unthinkable—that she would climb in with him and subdue her better judgment, her thoughts of what Arlen
would think of her abandoning her assigned tasks, and
go after all. He tilted his head back to look at her, his
smile fading while he waited for her to decide.

Myra realized she was glimpsing his hand, a card he
should have played closer to his chest—he badly wanted
her to go. Standing there in the moment of a simple ex-
change she'd fallen heir to a piece of insight that should
now constrain her, but after the instant of recognition
she buried the knowledge and erected a pretense of innocence that would allow her to go, because now, more
than anything, that was what she wanted.

She grinned. "Okay," she said, and walked around
the truck and got in. She slammed the door and they
drove up the hill, the empty trailer skating noisily behind them. Neal looked at her, grateful, but she denied
acknowledgment, looking away, saying casually, "What
are we doing?"

"I'm picking up Wilbur," said Neal, and he grinned
at her, tickled but apologetic in case she should think it
indelicate. But Myra smiled. She had heard about him:
Neal's 4-H bull the year he was sixteen, a bum, raised in
the barn, tame and hand-fed, grown into a docile, red-
and-white giant, transformed by biological imperative
each spring into a horny rogue, implacable as a tank. He
was on loan in Glendo to Arlen's brother John. As they
drove Neal told her the story.

John ran sixty cows on the school section across the
road from the old Dyer place. It was rough sagebrush
pastureland, cut by coulees and draws breaking to the
east into badlands where the Burrells summered their
registered Herefords. Both of John's young Red Angus
bulls had been sidelined earlier in the spring by polled
bull disease, causing a lot of amusement up and down
the creek, but raising for John the specter of half a herd
of dry cows. The Angus bulls lumbered energetically
among the cows with their belly whackers dragging in
the sage, until they hung limp and useless in swollen,

festering misery, and the bulls stood still, groaning their desire.

John hauled them to the vet who said one wasn't worth treating, he might as well make hamburger, and the other would need twice daily doctoring if there was to be any hope for the following year, and if he recovered, for God's sake keep the cows on the meadows until they were covered. John put the remaining bull in the corral and twice a day Lorraine and the boys helped run him into the chute, coming at him with arms flapping while he pawed dust up over his shoulders and swung his lowered head. He could spin and break past them in the small space with surprising agility, maddened by pain and progressively more savvy about avoiding the chute. When they succeeded in squeezing him into immobility John reached through the planks and cleaned the penis, scraping away the cracked, dust-encrusted scabs until it dripped blood and ran with the yellow antibiotic ointment. Lorraine couldn't watch and the three boys hopped away howling, clutching at their crotches in empathy.

One early morning in half light John saddled Babe and rode up through the school section to his tank where he climbed the windmill and sat in the exhilaration of height and dawn, the wind scudding pink-and-gray clouds low overhead and whirling the blades behind him, the pipes clanking and sucking. The road wound out of the hills on the ridge tops, following the path of the creek and its dark, wide snake of bordering trees folding among the convolutions of the terrain. The road dipped and straightened briefly in front of his own place where the tin roof of the barn reflected the sky with a watery glint, then disappeared eastward only to come back into view as it came out onto the flat, passed under the four-lane and teed up against the old highway. There were no cars in sight in either direction. John stood up then and looked behind him into the hills for a long time before climbing down.

Above the tank a barbed wire fence made an oblique angle and marched out of sight across the shoulder of the hill. The posts were widely spaced and shallowly planted in the rocky soil. Gray-and-orange lichen grew in the vertical grooves of the posts where the sapwood had eroded away into a rugged miniature topography. John planted his boot halfway up a post and pushed, and it sagged over with a rusty squeal as the surrounding spans of wire stretched and gave. It splintered off just above the dirt, leaving a stump of jagged teeth. Two more posts fell the same way, then John remounted. Babe skittered across the downed wire with her eyes rolling, snapping her hooves up in tight articulation in case the wire should spring up after her.

John rode through the badlands, winding up among the junipers and sand draws until he came upon the Burrell Herefords, their backs like liver islands in shoulder-high greasewood. He rode among them and eased a bull and two pairs (to make it look more plausible) out of the herd and moved them slowly out of the hills and down toward the school section. He pushed them across the downed fence and on until they joined up with his own cows.

The Burrells were indifferent fencers and John gambled that this semen rustling would never be known, or if discovered, that the Burrells would attribute the knocked-down fence to wind or winter drifts or the weight of cows yearning toward the water in John's tank. He knew, though, that the convenience of this solution to his predicament would raise suspicious eyebrows, so it was with relief that he accepted the loan of Wilbur when Arlen called and offered.

Arlen didn't like Wilbur. He was moving away from hybridizing with the colossal Semintals, and Wilbur was Neal's. The satisfaction of putting John in his debt and getting the beast off the place at the same time fell into his mind like balm, and Wilbur was hauled to Glendo and turned out with the cows. John pushed the Burrell bull back across the fence line with no one the wiser.

Between the Burrell bull and Wilbur all of John's cows were soon covered, but when his job was done in the school section Wilbur's indomitable ardor took him down the hill to the county road where he leaned on the fence, yearning across at the heifers pastured on the other side. The wire yielded to his weight, and John didn't know how long he'd been there when he discovered Wilbur riding a little black baldy that staggered under him. There was no telling how many heifers he'd bred, and John had visions of the vet boarding at their place next winter with no time to go home between cesareans; each calf, dead or alive, worth its weight in vet bills.

He beat the bull off with a board then stood by his pickup leaning on the horn, blaring his rage across the fields to summon Lorraine, and pitching rocks left-handed at the heifers to scatter them. Lorraine came flying through the horse pasture, surprisingly fleet in her duck-footed run, her breasts bobbing up under her chin. In her hurry she snagged herself on the barbed wire as she squeezed through the fence and John had to rescue her.

They had to drive the whole bunch to the barn, then cut Wilbur into the corral with the sick Angus. John called Arlen to say he was bringing the bull back and where should he put him, but Arlen wouldn't say.

The next day John was farming across the creek and all day he could hear Wilbur lowing mournfully, and pictured him, neck outstretched with strings of saliva streaming.

Late in the afternoon Wilbur put his head against the top plank of the corral gate and pushed until it splintered, then he reared back and cleared the remaining boards in an improbable hop, and strode across the barnyard, balls swaying, to the heifer pasture. John's boys saw him as he passed the bunkhouse window and they ran out and tried to turn him back, yelling and jumping around and hitting him with sticks, but Wilbur took no notice—taming him had taken his fear and he

couldn't be herded. It took John on Babe and Lorraine
and the boys on foot to return him to the corral a
second time. They repaired the gate and put Wilbur inside the barn and turned their backs on his bellows.

The next afternoon when John returned from across
the creek the barn door was down and Lorraine was in
tears. John was wild. Arlen was irrigating on the Wagonhound place when John called, and Florence couldn't
raise him on the radio, but John wouldn't hang up until
she went out to the shop to fetch Neal in. Neal had seldom heard John so angry, and though he couldn't listen
to the story without smiling, he was penitent and
ashamed as though Wilbur's rapaciousness reflected his
own nature.

Out by the airport, before they got onto the interstate,
Neal pulled in to a drive-up window and bought a half
case of Coors. He put it on the floor by Myra's feet.
"You want a beer?" he asked, leaning over to pull one
out, and looking up at her with his head at her knee.
She took it and he pulled another free for himself, and
they released the smell of hops and truancy into the cab.

They didn't talk all the way to Glendo. It was warm
for May and the sun dazzled through the pitted
windshield and lay on Myra's lap like a cat. Myra had a
talent, like disengaging from gear, for freewheeling in
the moment, without volition to turn events to her will.
She leaned her head back and sipped her beer while the
landscape spun by, having launched herself into the
afternoon accepting what would come without precon-
ceptions or responsibilities, like the dog in the back of
the pickup, forefeet braced on the edge of the bed,
squinting and grinning into the wind—along for the
ride.

A cottonwood windbreak ran along the driveway to the
tangled lilac hedge that enclosed the yard of the old

Dyer place. John and Lorraine lived in a second-hand
double-wide set up on cinder blocks out front in what
had been the horse pasture. Leona Dyer, Arlen and
John's mother—old, top-heavy, rolling through her last
years on silicone hips—still lived in the white, two-story
house behind the trees, an oasis of cool and shade
proclaiming a lost aesthetic.

Twenty years before, Ferris and the boys had painted
all the buildings—out buildings, sheds, house, and
barn—white, and the central yard was blinding even
after the decades of graying and peeling. It was con-
gested with an unbelievable assortment of cars, trucks,
and farm machinery that John traded for and bought at
auction, always thinking he'd fix up. He could make almost any machine run and he functioned as a parts sup-
plier to his neighbors and friends.

When Neal pulled in with the trailer clangoring behind him, a stream of dogs spilled out from under the
trucks and tractors, barking wildly, all bearing a familial
resemblance to one another in their wiry, roan coats and
erect tails and ears, heirs to a singular lineage. Neal
circled the yard and parked by the barn.

The dogs milled around as Neal and Myra got out,
then subsided back to their spots of shade as John came
out of the shop shouting at them. Neal put the carton of
beer on the hood of the truck and stood three fresh ones
around as John came up. John nodded and smiled and
opened a beer with a foamy hiss.

"Hi, Myra," he said. "I heard you were back."

"Hi, John." She hadn't seen him since he was a kid
and now he looked so like his father it was hard to
reconcile the beer in his hand.

They leaned on the truck in the prow of shade
thrown by the pitch of the barn roof. Behind them, behind the patched door, the barn resounded with a
mournful bellow from Wilbur. "Son of a bitch," said
John, "he's a goddamn fucking machine." But he was
grinning, and then he doubled over in laughter at
remembered images, and Neal laughed too. "You should

have seen him. Humping the heifers. I should have shot the son of a bitch." He straightened up. "Arlen must have been plumb tickled to send him down here. Doing me a favor." Neal grinned at him. "It's your fucking bull," said John, with an edge of sourness now, but not meant for Neal. "Let's get the son of a bitch in the trailer so we know where he's at."

Neal pulled the pickup and trailer forward, then backed up in line with the barn door. When they slid the door open Wilbur obligingly ambled into the trailer and it settled heavily down upon its wheels. Myra looked through the grillwork at him—a ton of bull, blowing warm, cowy breath out in a mild, raspy sigh, and flicking his tongue up to curl into his nostrils. Neal stepped onto the running board beside her and stuck his arm through the bars to rub him on his bony forehead, and the bull leaned into the caress like a cat.

They finished their beers then walked across the yard and through the gate to the house. They stepped up into a windowless, wooden porch that John had attached to the trailer. It was cluttered with generations of overshoes, coveralls, hats, gloves, and jackets, an upright freezer, a refrigerator, and a litter of puppies in a cardboard box. Myra was hit with a wall of heat and the stench of souring milk and dogs, and with the bagpipe drone of hundreds of captive flies. John took a six-pack of beer from the refrigerator and they went on in.

Here too the air was still and smelled of sour milk and rancid butter. Every surface was covered with dirty dishes and containers of leftover food, parts of the separator, overflowing ashtrays, and forgotten half-drunk glasses of iced tea attesting to a flow of visitors.

As they came in Lorraine sprang up from a bar stool at the kitchen counter with an energy that contradicted the surrounding evidence of sloth and despair, and lifted her face for John to kiss.

"Hi, honey," she said, and then, "Hi, Neal." Arlen and John had married sisters and she turned an armored

look on Myra that mirrored Florence, and they bobbed
heads.

They sat in the shambles of the kitchen at the formica bar and Neal and John talked in slow circles about
the weather, the prospects of hay, calving, and the
neighbors. Green chiffon curtains swagged limply before
double-glazed windows, distancing the pastures and sky
behind a chemical green scrim. Time rolled slowly forward through the six-pack and the afternoon.

The shadows were lengthening and the air was
cooler, and the killdeers swooping and diving for in-
sects, when they stepped out of the house into the evening to move the irrigating water in the upper meadow
across the creek.

Myra went with them, knowing she shouldn't, that
she should stay and help Lorraine with dinner, and fence
and spar in the small small-talk of women, but she didn't
want to. The hopelessness of making a meal in the dis-
order of Lorraine's kitchen, and the distance already between them, sent her out with the men.

She sat bracketed by their shoulders in the rough-
riding work pickup they called "grampa" because long
ago it had belonged to Ferris, their words washing
across her, rocking between them as the truck dipped
and bucked in the ruts, alive to their presence.

The boys, Vincent and Brian and Francis, stood in
back and John took the crossing fast to splash them, and
they shouted and banged thunder with their fists on the
roof of the truck. Neal turned laughing to look back at
them—himself only recently graduated to the cab.

They parked at the edge of the hay field, unbeliev-
ably green in the surrounding hills and sheeted under-
foot with water, and got out. John turned off the
sprinkler and they spread out across the field and marched
the sections of pipe upward toward the dry end of
the meadow, then fitted them together again and sent
the water coursing through the pipes and spitting out
across the young alfalfa once more. Myra had stayed
closest to the truck and she looked down the line of

pipe at John and Neal and the two big boys, and little
Francis—a line of Dyers of diminishing age spaced
across the field as they would be across the future, and
the pipe like the thread of connection running between
them all.

   Having shared the task, small though it was, drew
Myra closer into their circle. They stood around the
pickup and watched as the evening sun fled across the
field and climbed the eastern bluffs, leaving them in the
blue light of dusk. Overhead the killdeers looped in and
out of sunlight. John lingered, mellowed by the afternoon, happy to be there across the creek, out of earshot
of mother and wife, in his field with the abundance of
water at his feet. Myra thought that it was all worth it—
this was what she'd hoped for, to be a part of again—
and thankfulness and kinship swelled inside her like a
sigh, and gratitude to John for his easy inclusion of her.

   They got back in the truck and headed home, quiet
and bonded, then plunged into the squalor of the
kitchen, and of macaroni and chemical cheese.

It was dark when Neal and Myra left. John and the boys
walked them out and tried to hand a puppy through the
window to Myra, reaching in to drop it in her lap,
laughing as she pushed it back and rolled up the window. John pressed it against the glass and whined its imagined pleas. "Says, 'Please take me home.' Says, 'These
guys'll put me in a sack and throw me in the crick.'
Says, 'Come on, Myra.'" The bitch was dancing around
his legs and rearing up against the door to nuzzle the
puppy for reassurance. Neal gunned the truck and they
jerked away laughing, with Wilbur staggering for balance
in the trailer behind them.

   Neal glanced at Myra, a mile away at the other end
of the seat by the door, and wished for another pas-
senger to shift her closer to him. That afternoon when
they lurched together crossing the creek and her
shoulder grazed his arm, and her foot braced on the

floorboard beside his, knees bumping, he had yielded himself to the secret pleasure of the contact, all his sensations listing toward their shared boundary, safe in knowing his desire, like a perfect crime, was undetectable. He supposed that he could jolt against his neighbor in a pickup a thousand times and never give a passing thought to the touch, unless it was so sought and prized. Remorse for having used her unselfconscious presence overtook him, and he thought that his absurd fixation demeaned even her as its unwitting object. He would return her dignity by a scrupulous denial of his purloining desire.

Arlen pastured some old dry cows on a couple of sections out north of town that had belonged to his father—just grazing land, no buildings, no creeks or trees, just plains and a windmill. The whole neighboring countryside was a patchwork of pastures indistinguishable from one another, and further cut and complicated by a pipeline slashing across with fenced right-of-ways and infrequent gates. In the dark Neal had trouble finding where he was going—one gate in the barbed wire along the county road looked very much like another, and his sense of time and distance was muddled by his preoccupation with Myra. He finally decided he'd driven too far, and in a perilous maneuver turned the pickup and trailer in the narrow road, and backtracked to the most likely looking gate. They made slow and bumpy progress through the pasture up a faint track that Neal thought should lead to a tank. They found a windmill and tank and a salt lick beside it, and signs that cows had recently been there, but none in sight. Neal honked the horn, a sooey rolling out across the dark plains that in winter would bring them at a trot looking for hay, but fell on deaf ears now they fed on grass.

Neal and Myra got out and stood listening in the warm wind beneath the clanking windmill in the lights of the truck, with Wilbur's heavy movements shifting the trailer behind them.

"Well, let's try to find them," said Neal finally, and they got back into the truck and quartered the field, bouncing in the sagebrush, the lights probing the darkness. They were finally stopped by a dry ditch that the trailer couldn't cross. Neal got out again and stood in the sage, listening. He knew he shouldn't let Wilbur out alone, and there was a small nagging unease he was trying to ignore that this might not even be the right pasture. He knew he should find the cows and look at a brand to confirm that it was their field, and to assure, as much as he could, that Wilbur would stay put, but he was tired and it seemed hopeless to roam the prairie in the dark, and he felt Myra's eyes on his back in imagined impatience. He got back in and drove along the ditch looking for a spot where he could cross, driving faster, erratically, trying to out-distance his anxiety. Myra was braced against the bucking of the pickup with one hand on the seat between them and the other gripping the top of the window frame, and behind them the trailer slewed sideways with the impact of Wilbur's weight slung against the side. Wilbur swelled in Neal's mind, ballooning out of the confines of the trailer to loom above him like a cloud of guilt and bad judgment. He braked suddenly and came to a halt. "I'm letting him out," he said, and slid out before she could answer, leaving the motor running. Myra got out and watched Neal swing open the tailgate and flap his arms and rattle the bars to make the bull back up. When he stepped out Wilbur looked around and raised his nose in the wind, snuffling, and bawled—a long, lonesome, pained call of beastly yearning floating over the plains. Somewhere the cows may have heard, and listened, then returned to their grazing.

Neal had trouble finding the gate again that let them out onto the county road. He drove in aimless zigzags with no sense of direction until by chance he crossed the track to the windmill.

It was late before they finally descended the hill to home. When Neal came to a stop at the fence in front of

the house, Myra opened the door and slid out and
evaporated into darkness, closing the door on prospects
that in the afternoon had seemed limitless and unut-
terably cheering to Neal. Now the day was over, its
potential spent. It might be months or never before he'd
have her alone again. A lifetime's illusions can be built
on a few charged encounters and the intervals between
filled with fantasies of projected sympathy—lives twining together in a braid of crossed paths and separations.

Arlen caught Neal the next morning by the yard gate as
he went out for chores, shouting from the porch where
he stood in his socks.

"Hey!" Then a pause, while Neal turned around and
they sized each other up. "I don't want that bull up
there. Jesus Christ. You know what's going to happen.
He's not going to stay in a pasture full of drys. He's
going to go through fences 'til he finds someone else's
heifers to hump. That was John's problem down there.
He was lucky to have the son of a bitch. You don't go
taking a half day off chasing around the goddamned
country doing something that's none of your goddamned business."

Neal pictured the whole ranch leaning in with
cupped ears to listen. He refused to be drawn into it and
stood still waiting for his father to be done. After a moment Arlen started up again.

"What in the hell were you thinking? I can't believe
it, taking Myra with you. The two of you, off for half a
day, doing something that's up to John. He wants the
fucking bull and then he doesn't want him. Well, Jesus,
what are we supposed to do? To and fro with the son of
a bitch 'til John's satisfied? He ought to be goddamned
pleased that his cows are covered. You remember something, Neal—you're working for me."

Neal carried the argument on in his head all morning—all that he could say in defense of himself
countered by the chimera of his father's logic—until

finally he admitted defeat, loathing himself for a
Frankenstein that had reared Wilbur and loosed him,
and there was no undoing the damage. This thought
came to him as he stood in the horse corral with his out-
stretched hand reaching to pull trust from Clay, and he
wondered if his good intentions would always lead to
calamity.

Arlen saw him there and took it as a further affront,
shouting, "Neal, for Christ's sake what the hell are you
doing now?" as he stamped by and went over to his
truck, bony and . angular, lost in his clothes, his
shoulders hiked and rounded in a consumptive curl
around his chest, his movements swift and purposeful.
Myra came out of the barn in time to hear his shout and
watch his going. He seemed sad in his rage, and frail,
and she had an unguarded urge to comfort him. As he
drove away she lifted her hand and waved.

Arlen saw her wave from the corner of his eye and it
was almost enough to turn him back. As he drove up the
hill he saw her in the rearview mirror, watching him
from the barn door, but he drove on, the gravel spitting
from under the tires. All day he carried the image of her
with him—lips parted as though to call out to him, and
her hand raised, and he took a small pleasure from the
thought that she'd wished to detain him and he hadn't
stopped.
     He saw Valerie on the road, headed for town, and
they slowed and stopped, the two pickups nosing
together, and when he asked her to, she turned around
and preceded him back to her place where they tumbled
together into her unmade bed.
     Arlen was always ashamed in daylight when he made
love to Valerie. He felt himself laughable in his bony
white nakedness and need, but Valerie never seemed to
notice. She sprawled before him in the cool light of

morning, completely what she was, while a part of him
stayed detached and watched in humiliation. She had no
shame herself, not about the rumpled bed and unwashed
dishes, or about her doughy stomach and pendant
breasts, and it was this ease about herself that was most
seductive to him.

Valerie drank a beer with him afterward in the
kitchen, warm and damp and satisfied. She sat on the
counter and swung her feet and grinned at him. She
knew she drove him wild and she laughed in good-
humored disbelief at his attempts to claim her. She knew
it was a torment to want her so, and she thought that
she might wear him down until someday he'd marry her
if nothing better had come along for her.

Arlen sat in the kitchen, as familiar to him as his
own after years of visiting Valerie, his boots crunching
in the crumbs on the speckled linoleum floor, locked in
the misery of his thoughts of Neal and the bull and the
flame of Myra. He reached for his hat and drained his
beer and strode out, Valerie erased now by other pre-
occupations. But she followed him to the door, and
when he turned as he got into his truck he saw her leaning against the jam, soft and complacent, and he was
wanting her again before he was out of the yard.

Neal and Myra had released the bull in the right pasture,
but by the time Arlen found him the next afternoon he'd
gone through three fences and was grazing with a herd
of registered Herefords. Arlen's first thought was to
shoot him where he stood, drop him at short range with
the 30.06 and watch him go down slowly on buckling
knees and feel the earth shake as he landed. His hand
was already on the rifle when he controlled the impulse.
He spent the next hours in an increasingly foul humor
driving the reluctant bull ahead of the pickup, patching
fence as he went.

Wilbur's normally placid temperament was strained
by the exercise of being herded, and by the time Arlen

got him through the last fence and back where he belonged the bull was swinging his lowered head and turning on the vexatious truck, pawing clouds of dust up over his shoulders. Arlen put the pickup between himself and the bull when he got out to splice the wire.

Unsure of how long he could count on Wilbur to stay put, Arlen drove into town and called home from the Daylight Doughnut. He stood at the pay phone against the back wall, jigging with anger and white around the lips. "Find Neal and tell him to get out north and get that goddamned bull out of my life and off my place!" There was silence as he listened to Florence on the other end. "I don't give a shit. Find him. And tell him to bring posts—he's going to have to fix fence. And tell him to come alone." Arlen hung up and sat down. The counter girl had to turn away to hide her smile. He gulped his coffee, burning his tongue in his haste.

Florence called repeatedly on the radio but couldn't raise Neal, or Tom either. They probably had the radio in the truck turned off, or weren't even in the truck. She couldn't remember where they were that day. She probably hadn't ever known. It irked her—Arlen never told her anything and then when something went wrong she was supposed to be clairvoyant.

She went out and knew immediately that she would be cold despite the sunshine, but instead of going back in for a jacket she hurried on, wrapping her arms across her chest. She hoped Neal would be in the shop, although she knew it was unlikely since she didn't see his pickup, and he wasn't. There were no trucks around the barns either, but she went in anyway, stepping into the fragrant dusk of the loft. She stood in wonder for a few minutes looking at a cat with thirteen kittens in a nest of hay. Their barn cats were tame, not the disappearing shadows of most ranches, and the mother cat looked up at her through slitted eyes and curled her paws into ecstatic fists, her purr rattling in the silence.

Florence climbed down the ladder and went through the milking barn to the calving shed, and then on out into the corrals. She heard hammering and knew someone was around, but almost turned back, unseen, to go home when she saw it was Myra rebuilding a feed bunk in the small corral. Then Myra turned and saw her, her mouth full of nails, and for a moment Florence looked at her with a man's eyes.

Myra was mystified by Florence's presence, not sensing any haste or purpose. She spit the nails into her hand and climbed down, and the two women sat side by side on the edge of the feed bunk in the sun.

After a little silence Florence said, "There's a cat in there with thirteen kittens."

Myra smiled, not wanting to contradict, and said gently, "They're not all hers. There's another mama cat and they both nurse them all."

Florence looked at her. "You're kidding."

Myra shook her head and they smiled at each other, liking the cats' maternal arrangement, and inspired by it with a warmth for each other. They relapsed into silence. Florence's feet, shod in two-eyelet sneakers and anklets, hardly reached the ground, and Myra felt rough beside her, her own feet in mud-caked boots.

"Where's Neal today?" Florence asked after a while.

Guilt washed over Myra, and fear of some ungovernable transparency—a flush, or a twitch beneath her eye—that would give her away and launch Florence at her face with bared talons to rend the imagination that robbed her first of her husband and now of her son. But nothing must have showed for Florence went on. "Arlen called from town having fits about that bull."

"I think they're discing and ditching at the Lindmeir place," Myra said. She wondered how bad Arlen would make it for Neal. He'd said nothing to her.

"They won't answer the radio," said Florence. "I don't think they ever have it on. It makes me so mad.

Now I've got to go over there in the car." But she continued sitting, banging her heels against the planks. "The
sun feels good—here out of the wind." After a while she
sighed and stood up. "Well. See you later," she said.
Myra watched her walk across the corral and back into
the barn.

It was dusk by the time Neal got out to the north pasture and found Wilbur, and he had trouble loading him.
He pushed him into a corner but couldn't run him into
the trailer—the bull only blinked mildly at Neal's flapping arms—until finally, as though the notion of what
was wanted had only just penetrated, he stepped ami-
ably in of his own accord. Neal replaced two broken fence
posts with metal ones, standing on the fender of the
pickup and driving them into the rocky hardpan with a
sledge hammer—a mythic silhouette against the setting
sun if there'd been anyone to see.

He took Wilbur to Guernsey to the sale barn and unloaded him into a pen in the maze of corrals and lanes
and gates, and stood in the starlight and rubbed the
bull's bony poll with his knuckles in farewell. The next
Friday he sold to a flat-land breeder from Nebraska for
eighteen hundred dollars and Neal was glad he hadn't
gone to the killers. He bought a stereo cassette player
for his pickup.

Arlen seemed over his pique after the bull was gone
from the place, and he laughed when he heard that Wilbur had sold to a breeder, envisioning the problems he'd
be causing for someone else, but the whole incident was
another tap on the wedge between Neal and Arlen.

Chapter Fourteen

Florence was cutting up fryers one afternoon when Neal paid her a totally uncharacteristic visit, coming in with the outdoors trapped in his clothes, the door banging behind him. He kept his jacket on and sat down with his legs stretched out in her path between the table and the sink, and pushed back his cap and smiled at her. She felt an engulfing, tender exasperation for him. Here he sat, unaccustomed, in her kitchen in the middle of the day, so much a man and yet she could hardly believe he was old enough to drink coffee. "What are you doing here?" she asked, roughly tender like a cat's tongue.

"Visiting you," was his answer, grinning.

She wiped her hands and poured him a cup of left-over breakfast coffee and looked at him as she set it down, suddenly scared that something had happened, that he was here to tell her something awful. The fear strained her voice when she asked, "Where's your dad?" Had they fought? Was he leaving? Florence knew that Neal should leave, that living here and working for Arlen was wrong for him, but the prospect of him gone filled her with such emptiness she knew she'd fight to keep him on. She seldom saw him—he came in for

meals and ate in silence and then was gone— but the
knowledge of his presence consoled her.

"I don't know. Don't worry. Don't you want me
here?" he answered, and she turned back to the chickens, reassured.

She thought that Neal was so dear to her and so
wounded by circumstance, she suddenly turned back to
him and embraced him, her wet hands behind his head.
He ducked out of her grasp, laughing. "Ma, you're all
bloody." She leaned over and kissed his forehead, then
turned back to the chickens. He sat for a long time in
silence before he finally asked, "Ma, what's Myra to
me?"

Though her back was to him she'd been listening
with her whole body, waiting to learn why he'd come,
fearing his resentment, dreading the loss of him, and she
heard his question as reassuringly conversational. She
looked at him. What was Myra to any of them? But she
thought about it and said, "I think she's your first cousin
once removed. Maybe your second cousin. I'm never
sure. Why?"

He didn't meet her eyes. "I just wondered."

Florence looked at him. With the smile gone from
his face his features fell into a gentle, downward slant. It
pierced her that in repose he should look despondent.
She thought of the little boy that years ago she had shut
out of her kitchen, evening after evening, while she
cooked. He had wailed and pounded on the door and
flung himself against it, but she'd closed her ears and
heart to him. She wondered now that she could have
done it, but she'd been young and overworked, on Twin
Pine cooking for the men, and that, three times a day,
and Neal too, was more than she could manage. When
the meals were over and cleared away she opened the
door and he fell in against her, catching his breath in
shuddering gasps, his outrage spent. But she thought he
never leaned on her again with confidence, and he se-
questered his need away from her.

Neal watched her, her hands shiny and white and sure
with the knife and the chickens, until he had to turn his
eyes away, seeing the birds as they had been, right side
up with their feathers on, pecking and scratching, stupid
but quick, and lying now on their backs in a pile, naked
in their loose, yellow skin, hacked into pieces under his
mother's blade. It chilled him to watch her mother's
hands of kindness and comfort merciless with the chickens. He looked into the thin coffee in his cup and
swirled it, trying to work out the dilution of great-
grandfather Patrick Dyer's genes flowing in his and
Myra's veins. He got up and Florence said quickly,
"Don't go," but he only smiled and tugged his cap
down over his forehead and went out.

Myra went to the Colby's branding with Florence. Arlen
and Neal and Tom had gone over early, before light, to
help gather the cattle. Myra was sorry she had said she'd
go. It was a Saturday and she wouldn't have had to.
Arlen hadn't mentioned it—it had been Florence the
morning before when Myra brought in the milk, saying,
with her odd, challenging, direct look, "You can go
over to the Colby's branding with me tomorrow if you
want." Myra had said yes and almost immediately
wished she hadn't. She knew it meant she'd go as one of
the women, bringing a dish, to visit and serve and clean
up, and play the charade of being one of them.

That evening she mixed cinnamon rolls and set
them to rise overnight, and baked them in the morning
and carried them, hot and fragrant, up the lane—a tith-
ing to convention.

They drove in silence, going south on the county
road and then west into the hills along a slimmer, tum-
bling La Bonte fringed with aspen, the leaves coming out
in a mist of pale green hearts.

Myra followed Florence into the house and it was as
she had feared. The women sat in soft, immobile
mounds around the front room, arms folded, eyes and

tongues flickering, like toads in ambush. Florence made
a round of introductions, and Myra ducked and bobbed
at each appraising face, hating every one, and herself for
the hypocrisy of her own smile. She put her rolls down
on the end of the laden table in the kitchen and stood in
the doorway.

When Florence next looked for her Myra had
evaporated, and through the old wavery glass of the
paned window Florence could see her crossing the yard
toward the barns and corrals, and a little corner of her
own capitulated soul saluted her, captive of convention
no more.

Around the corrals the air was thick with dust and bitter
with the stench of burning hair. The cows bawled, over-
lapping continuous bellowing, and the ignited propane
that heated the irons roared, and the world closed down
under a dome of sound. Myra leaned on the corral fence
and watched the calves singled out and roped and
hauled by a heel, scrabbling and bleating, to be lifted
and flung down and knelt on, stretched and braced,
their eyes rolling like milky blue marbles. It was a three-
iron brand, multiplying the torture, then the heifers
were up, but the little bulls' balls were frayed away and
growth hormones implanted in their ears, and when
released they lay still a moment, doubting their freedom,
before springing up and trotting into the safety of their
numbers, trying to shake away the pain in a spatter of
blood.

   Neal was roping. He rode through the calves at a
walk, his loop at his side, and they spread away from
him like a retreating tide, and then suddenly, with a
whirl and an underhand flick he'd have one by the heel.

   The teamwork was swift and practiced, except for a
woman with spreading hips and a cheerful, maddening
incompetence. Myra watched her, the only other

woman, wondering why she was tolerated, picking her
exclamations out of the clamor. As she watched, so
quickly she couldn't say what happened, a struggling
calf loosened a hind leg from the woman's grasp and it
flashed forward in an outward arcing kick that struck
Arlen flush in the face as he bent above it. He went over
backward, blood blossoming from his nose. The calf was
up, scrambling at the end of the rope. Myra suppressed
an impulse to slip through the fence and hasten to Arlen,
and her fingers bit into the wood as she watched him
regain his feet and hold a blue bandana against his face.
He swayed, but from the way he turned and nodded and
the jocular expressions of the other men, she concluded
he was all right. Someone handed him his hat. The
woman stood beside him and rose on her toes to kiss
the cheek he bent to her, then she squeezed through the
poles of the corral and came along the fence toward
Myra.

She stopped where Myra stood and slapped at the
dust and dung on her jeans then brushed her hands
together, looking at Myra and working a piece of gum
around the back of her mouth. "Did you see that?" she
asked. Myra nodded. "Busted his nose I'll bet, poor darling. He'll be sore tomorrow. Sore at me too," and she
laughed, an easy, bubbling, careless laugh. "I'm Valerie
Pruitt," she said. "Who are you?"

Myra told her, watching closely to see if it meant
anything to her, and it didn't. Myra watched her walk
toward the house. That was her. She looked back across
the corral at Arlen and his eyes were on her, and even
with the bandana covering the lower part of his face she
could read confirmation there.

The work resumed and Neal rode over, dancing a
sizzling nut in his hand—ritual fare cooked on the oil
drum surrounding the propane fire—and teased her to
eat it, but she had no stomach for it. He did then, white
teeth biting, grinning at her, while his horse laid back its
ears and stepped in place, eager to work again.

At noon Myra followed the men in and watched them wash their hands and arms in a tub on the porch and splash their faces, and then go in to fill their plates and slide out again to stand in the yard around a bathtub filled with ice and beer.

The women laughed and mothered Arlen when he came in, the blade of his nose pale and softened with swelling and both eyes already blue in the corners. Florence stood back, relinquishing proprietorship, and let them cluck, but when it came out how it had happened, Myra saw the glance that flew between them and saw Florence's face shut down.

Myra washed dishes then, until Florence was ready to go, looking out through the curtains over the sink at the circle around the bathtub. A little boy, on a dare, slipped among the forest of blue jeans to swipe a beer and carried it off behind the lilacs to share around with his friends in triumph.

She rode home with Florence, united in unspoken league against Valerie Pruitt. Why her, Myra wondered— pear-shaped in a flamingo tank-top—what was the need she filled?

Chapter Fifteen

The trail, the annual move to summer pasture, started one late May morning at four-thirty, long before the sun. As the years on La Bonte and the Wagonhound passed, Arlen had groomed his bottomland, scraped meadows out of hillsides, ditched, and engineered until he could water enough oats and alfalfa and brome and timothy hay to winter three times the cows that he had pastureland to summer. He bought sixteen sections of prairie a hundred miles southwest, across the first gentle rising of the Rockies, and it was to there that every spring he trailed a thousand head of cattle, all his pairs and yearlings, every head on the place except for the old drys out north and a few cows with calves too young to make the journey. It looked like a gallant anachronism, a salute to the Old West, but Arlen had worked out on paper the savings in grass and fuel and hours and wages, without sentimentality.

They saddled up in confusion in the darkness of the calving shed and rode up the hill with the soft clatter of bare hooves on the dirt of the road, the horses held in, head-high and short-strided with eagerness. The predawn wind caught them at the top of the hill and they let the horses go a bit.

The cattle were held across the road in a half-section
pasture, darker shapes in the darkness heaving to their
feet and moving away from the horses, leaving behind
warm beds of flattened grass. The riders circled along
the fence line, then moved in, pushing them toward the
gate. An occasional hoot floated on the wind—one of
the boys urging them on. As the sky lightened Myra
could see the confluence of dark backs ahead as the
cattle bunched at the gate and spilled through. Arlen sat
his horse in the road counting them through the gate,
passing pebbles from hand to hand to keep track of the
hundreds.

The first miles were on the oiled county road,
downhill, and the cattle fanned out between the fences
in a dense, lowing phalanx. It remained cool with high,
feathery cirrus paling the sky and the scent of the Platte
on the wind. Florence drove out and took the riders
home in relays for breakfast. Bonnie was riding, taking a
week off from the First National, and Myra had gone the
day before with Neal to borrow horses in Glendo and to
pick up John's boys, swelling the crew to eight.

They'd found them all in the kitchen, packed in like kip-
pers in the heat, drinking beer and negotiating the sale
of a '57 Chevy hardtop to a college boy from Laramie
who had come over with a pole cutter John knew, and
two tanned girls in shorts. The girls were driving John
wild, all that leg and crazy over cowboys. The kid could
hardly believe he was going to get the Chevy for seven-
teen hundred dollars, but John was balking at a Nebraska
check, and they sat stalemated.

When they all trooped out to load the kids and
horses, clouds were piling up over the mountains
darkening the sky to the west, and a fresh little wind
was turning over the cottonwood leaves. The pole cutter and the kid from Laramie took a blanket and a six-
pack and led the girls down the creek under the trees to
wait out John's indecision. John's boys, Brian and Vin-

cent and Francis, made disorganized trips between the house and the pickup with their duffle bags and unwinding sleeping bags. Neal threw the saddles in on top with spread fenders to runnel the rain if it came. They loaded two horses and the boys piled in back on top of their gear, surrounding the gooseneck, and Myra and Neal got in and pulled away. Lorraine stood at the gate and waved, a cigarette between her fingers.

They drove on up the creek under the spreading rim of cloud to pick up a horse for Francis from John and Arlen's sister Rosemary. She was the oldest; a big-boned, graceless woman with indoor skin and an invalid petulance, who had jumped as a girl, when fortune smiled, to marry Ray Macky, a cowboy from east of the river with a walleye and, at thirty, false teeth and a head smooth and white as an egg on top. He'd leaned into the collar of ambition for her, and they had built a sixty-cow outfit up on the creek that in a good year made the land payment and bought a new pickup or swather, put braces on the kids' teeth and sent them to college. Arthritis stiffened and skewed Rosemary's hands and cortisone puffed her. Some days she never got out of her housecoat. Ray treated her like a jewel, fastening buttons and shampooing her head under the kitchen faucet with gentle fingers, and conspiring with her in the public fiction that things were otherwise, rising most mornings from the couch to make his own coffee and carry a cup in to her along with the first four aspirins of the day.

Ray raised big-barreled, gentle horses that would walk up and stick their heads into halters for a handful of oats.

Rosemary didn't even come to the door and wave as they stood in the yard after loading the horse, and her censure crept out from the house, coiling around Myra's ankles, stiffening her up with guilt and defensiveness. Rosemary had an elephant's memory and Myra knew that she lived in infamy in Rosemary's mind as an infant Circe entrancing Arlen, running with him hand in hand, fleeing a big sister's entreaties to "Wait up, you guys!"

Neal tried to get Ray to drink a beer, but he wouldn't, and Myra imagined that he entrusted his horse to them with misgiving.

The rain started before they even got back to town, big, slow drops that raised dust as they struck, and Neal stopped the truck and let the boys crowd into the cab, wedging Myra up against his ribs. She could feel his breathing and smell the musk of his skin. If she'd inclined her head she could have brushed his shoulder with her cheek.

They passed the '57 Chevy abandoned on the viaduct over the railroad tracks on the south side of Glendo, and waved when they saw the quartet from Laramie standing in the shelter of the pumps at the Standard station. They hadn't made it far. Myra wondered if the Nebraska check would clear.

It was dark when they got home. They unloaded the horses into the corral and listened to the confusion of squeals and thumps as they were initiated into the hierarchy of the ranch horses.

The miles unwound slowly behind the cattle. Arlen stayed at the head of the herd, riding point in the old parlance, his horse walking easily alongside the steers, up and back, opposite Neal on the other side. Tom and Vincent were paired behind them, one on either side, riding swing, and Bonnie and Francis rode on the flanks of the herd. The calves bunched in the drag, tired and wanting to turn back, so that the herd stretched ever thinner and longer from its crawling tail where Myra and Brian rode in hooting crisscrossings in the bar pits, willing the calves forward. If pressed too hard they escaped sideways, plunging through the fences to trot along on the other side of the wire until stopped by a corner where they ran in bewildered ells until someone rode back to chase them on foot, and fear persuaded them to scramble through the wire again.

Twelve miles in a twelve-hour day, much of it spent in interminable waits while the cattle fed and paired again with their calves. The horses were hobbled or grazed loose, bridle reins tied up around their ears, or were tied stamping to the fences.

Florence pulled a seventeen-foot travel trailer out to the plains, leapfrogging with the cattle as she advanced and halted for nooning or the night, a rolling bivouac to cook in, eat in, play cards in, sleep in on inclement nights packed in like sardines, head to foot with no thought to privacy, and to leave out on the plains, wired down against the wind, a makeshift summer head-quarters.

At noon they sat in the trailer beside the road eating lunch—bologna and processed cheese on white bread spread with Miracle Whip and margarine, Kool-Aid to wash it down. Florence wouldn't let the kids in. They stayed outside chucking rocks at the cows that stood in a foolish, belligerent line looking longingly back at where they'd come from, swelling udders reminding them of misplaced calves left in some remote corner of memory. Every now and then one escaped, breaking past the trailer window in a bag-swinging trot, and Arlen bellowed and Brian or Vincent caught up a horse and tore after it, whooping, to turn it back before the trickle became a flood of misguided maternal frenzy.

As she watched through the window Myra saw a cow and calf pair up, their panic evaporating. The calf swung in to suck, its tail flicking. Myra wondered how they recognized each other—sight or smell or the par-ticular sound of bawling? In a hybridized herd like this, did the mother of a blue baldy search among the calves, sniffing hopefully only at the blue baldies? Or was she as likely to think that a piebald or Charlais might be hers? Whatever keyed it, the recognition was categorical and immediate, and the cows, otherwise so muddled and foolish, accepted only their own. Myra imagined the relief of the reunion, the sighing away of loss and terror as the universe reassembled.

That evening they camped along the road where it
crested a long hill. During the night the cattle would
graze downhill, creeping westward untended. Already
the herd was distant, pushed onward after supper by the
kids on foot.

Neal stood in the road on the yellow line, the
highest point for miles, and showed Myra how to rope,
the descending sun stretching their shadows over the
crest of the hill to join the advancing evening. He shook
out a loop and whirled it above his head, spun by his
gyrating wrist, then hurled overhand, like a baseball. He
stood behind her and mimed the motions with her,
empty-handed in slow motion, his fingers gripping her
arm below the wrist to guide her, then pressing flat her
upturned palm, glancing at her sidelong and serious as
he coached her. Tom and Vincent swirled around them,
their own ropes singing in the air and snaking out along
the blacktop in pursuit of Francis acting the calf among
them, heeled over and over.

Myra stood beside Neal, her head bent as he showed
her how to shake the rope out of a figure-eight twist,
when Tom's loop sank around them and jerked them
against each other in an involuntary clinch. They struggled to get free, staggering together with pinioned arms,
while Tom backed up laughing, keeping the line taut.
Neal freed his hands enough to grasp the rope where it
led away from the hondo and he secured enough slack
to duck out of the loop, and Myra stepped free as it
dropped around her ankles. Then they dueled, Neal and
Tom, their whirling loops colliding in midair then
quickly coiled to sail out again until, spent with
laughter, they subsided and wound their ropes with deft
twists into sleeping circles to ride against their thighs
tied to their pommels.

The darkness fell quickly when the last of the sun
was gone from the sky. Myra leaned against her saddle
wrapped in her sleeping bag and wondered what he had
felt, snugged up against her. She had yielded, leaning
into him, her teeth grazing the arch of his collarbone as

she laughed, living every point of contact until she'd stepped dazed from the loop of rope. Now she would seek the touch of his fingers with "Please pass the salt," and absorb details of him that she could conjure at will—downward curve of snuff-black lips and hooded eyes, glint of teeth smooth and white as soap—but he'd never know, she reassured herself, would not have the arrogance to guess. She could reel with the impact of his eyes, create for herself the sensation of falling, of leaving her insides behind, her heart flying out her throat, like the weightless apex in a speeding car when it crests a hill, butterflies—an addicting, intoxicating rush—a clandestine thrill he'd never divine.

Myra lay back in her sleeping bag with her eyes wide open and swam in the canopy of stars and lost her own minutiae among the light years.

Chapter Sixteen

B lue flax nodded belly high and showered petals like flakes of sky at their passing. They were riding in sunshine under a clear, azure sky but to the west rolling black clouds were spilling over the hills. There would be no escape. Already Myra could smell the ozone and hear the thunder. In the pasture beside them a Belgian stallion galloped with massive grace, bugling a challenge or entreaty, aroused by the passing herd and impending storm. Their loose saddle horses sprinted along the fence and the cattle surged away from them. The air was suddenly cold under towering clouds. Myra stopped and untied her poncho and put it on, a blue, plastic shroud flapping in the wind that her horse wanted to spring from under. She rode low in the ditch in fear of lightning. When the rain started the horses traveled sideways with their necks arced leeward, legs scissoring, elegant as dressage mounts, their eyes blinking shut.

Neal had an ankle-length, yellow slicker, split up the back with a pleat to cover the cantle, but it was miles back in the pickup when the storm broke. Francis had left his rain jacket at home and he sobbed onward, enveloped in cold and misery. Myra couldn't think what to

do for him, but Neal rode back and dismounted and
took the little boy down from his horse and walked
with him in the road behind the cattle, hand in hand,
the horses following dark and wet at the ends of their
reins. Neal sang a tuneless verse from an old herding
song—"It's cloudy in the west and it looks like rain, and
my durned old slicker's in the wagon again." Francis
didn't smile but walked on in teeth-chattering wretched-
ness, hunched in his soaked windbreaker, the brim of
his straw hat descending around his ears. This episode
would join others in the log of history that gave him ego
and identity and challenged him to live out his own
myth.

Myra wondered at her inability to comfort the child,
half-dry and only half-miserable herself, and felt herself
reproached by Neal's example. They walked on, their
faces bluing with cold, until a car emerged from the
parting herd and Neal cavorted in its path, waving his
arms like semaphores, trying to make Francis laugh, then
snatched him up and squeezed into the back seat with
him to go back for his pickup. Myra thought longingly
of the heat that would slowly thaw them and dry their
clothes, but was warmed herself by the sun of Neal's
smile as he leaned out the car window and handed her
the reins of the horses to lead, saying, "I've got a pint in
the pickup," a promise to keep her going.

The electrical storm moved on and left a numbing driz-
zle in its wake. Neal and Francis came back in the pickup, bringing lunch sent by Florence, a big tupperware
tub filled with byrocks, rolls baked around a meat and
onion filling, but, oh shattering disappointment, frozen
solid, all their goodness locked away.

They passed the pint, holding it aloft out of reach of
the clamoring kids, and stood hopefully around the pickup with the hood up and the motor running, byrocks
poised on the manifold—an improbable field oven. Little
bits of dough softened and stuck to the metal, but the

engine's heat wasn't enough to penetrate to the frozen core.

"Kill the cook," said Arlen, but he was grinning. The disappointment pulled him closer to Bonnie and Neal in shared memories of past anticipations dashed at the dinner table by Florence's cooking.

They stood stiff-legged and still, for any movement brought new contact with wet jeans, conducting away body heat. Finally there was nothing to do but swing up into the wet saddles and ride onward into the afternoon in hopes of returning sunshine.

"From Cheyenne to Douglas, all the ranges I've rode," sang Arlen in a reedy baritone, and smiled at Myra. "That's all I know." Her heart flip-flopped in her chest. Where had his dourness flown, replaced by giddy amiability? Did the loss of creature comforts ease him away from thoughts of more complex adversity? Here was an Arlen to cherish, grinning in his red beard and sodden sheepherder's hat. She thought a nip more often wouldn't hurt, relieving him of his burden of self-denial. But what a puppy she thought herself, dancing on the string of his truculence, ready to pant after him when he smiled.

He transmitted energy to his horse and it swung away in a long-strided walk. His arm rose and fell against his thigh over and over, urging the cattle into motion. The line of his song floated back, sung again and again.

Later, when Florence nudged through the herd pulling the trailer, they hooted and booed and Neal pelted the truck with pocketed, frozen byrocks. She laughed without remorse and passed out handfuls of Halloween candy bars in consolation.

The next day the sun shone again and Myra, who had thought she'd never be warm, was hot, longing for a canteen and a bath. The wind sucked the moisture right up out of the earth and dust rose behind the cattle. They

had left the pavement and begun a long ascent that
would finally level off in a sweep of open rangeland.

Where a belt of crested wheat grass swooped off the
hills and spread in the barrow pits, they stopped to let
the cattle graze and pair up. There was no getting them
past it anyway.

Myra hobbled her horse with a figure eight of
rawhide and watched him hop in among the cows to
graze, his hind legs spread for stability, teeth tearing at
the grass. She wondered how they recognized the
crested wheat—its silvery shimmer in the wind, or a
fragrance she couldn't detect? Whatever it was they had
run the last hundred yards for it at a lumbering trot with
out-stretched noses and swinging bags.

Myra slipped through the fence and walked through
the sagebrush to an irrigation ditch that came off a creek
and angled across the pasture. She pulled her boots off,
rocking them heel to toe like a stuck car to get her hot
feet to let loose of them, rolled her socks off her toes
like hose, and sank her feet gratefully into the water.
Her shins bent obliquely away from her knees, blue and
flat and magnified under water, and the heat flooded
away. When she stood up in the ditch the surrounding
sagebrush towered shoulder high and she walked up and
down in a narrow canyon, the mud of the bottom
squishing between her toes and fouling the stream.
Glimpses of the road where Neal and Tom and Bonnie
and the kids sprawled in a circle playing Crap on Your
Neighbor blinked between the sage. Arlen had taken the
pickup and gone up the road to visit George Hughes.
The cows weren't even trying to get back. Myra climbed
out onto the bank again and stripped off her clothes sitting down, and slid back into the ditch naked. You'd
have to be on top of her before you'd see her. She
floated on her back in the current, hanging on to a stem
of sagebrush, the water rifling around her, her eyes on
the river of blue overhead. Below her the silt forgot her
feet and arranged itself back into ridges and whorls.
After a while she climbed out, sleek and white except

for the tan of her hands and her face and throat, and the
new sunburn on her arms. She pulled on her T-shirt and
underpants and slicked back her hair, then sat on the
edge of the ditch with her feet in the water, and smoked
a cigarette.

When Myra slipped back through the fence, Neal was
bent in the angle of a stranger's car door, his elbows
resting along the vee made by the roof and the top of
the door, his body a suppliant curve toward the girl sitting sideways behind the wheel of the red Camaro, her
knees grazing his.

Tom had flopped onto his back with his head in the
scattered cards and his hat over his face. Bonnie
cushioned her head on his stomach. "Who's that?" Myra
asked the blind moons of their faces. She had an impulse
to kick dust over their stupor.

"Julie Hughes," said Tom through his hat.

"Neal's sweetheart," said Bonnie in a carrying
singsong without opening her eyes.

Myra looked at Neal when she passed the car as she
walked up the road to retrieve her horse, and ached
with him for whatever youthful pain was between him
and the girl, so intense and simple, and so to be desired
when her own pain lay on her with the weight of the
humiliation of aging—she'd never play the girl to his
man. She heard the car start up behind her and watched
over her shoulder as it leaped away, and in a few moments Neal overtook her, cantering along the fence, his
face averted, and she knew she didn't exist for him. In
the ardor of his loss she offered no consolation.

Leona drove out from Glendo to picnic with them
where they camped in a bend of the La Prele. With a
powdery kiss she accepted Myra into her vague,
beneficent embrace of the past, old animosities forgotten, and rocked on her arm across the pasture to sit by
the fire in a folding lawn chair behind the cushiony
prow of her bosom, cooking a hot dog on a stick, an

anomaly in her flowered afternoon dress. She brought
treats from town, ice cream and doughnuts, and
Francis's raincoat, and came without expectations, out
of duty to tradition—an expedition to the edge of
civilization to carry back to her parlor and display over
tea and bridge like a beaded moccasin or a stick of
petrified wood, a trophy from the wilderness.

They ate standing up in a shifting circle around the
fire as the smoke plagued them—a picnic of obligation.
"I'm going to town," said Neal. "Grandma forgot beer,"
he added in answer to looks from Tom and Arlen, carrying different messages. He bent and kissed Leona and
then was hustling toward his pickup.

Myra was after him, calling "Neal!" without thought.
She caught him with his hand on the ignition and their
eyes met for a paralyzing moment. Why had she run
after him? What did she want? To go with him? To hold
him back? She stood beside the pickup, shocked, and
laughed breathlessly. "Cigarettes," she said, the first
thing that sprang to mind. "A carton. I'll pay you back."
He nodded and pulled away.

"Cigarettes," she said again, by way of explanation
to the carefully blank faces that turned toward her when
she returned to the fire. She'd teetered on the precipice
there, but had recovered and the rush of adrenalin subsided.

Myra thought of the long drive to town in the dusk,
his radio wailing, his heart on the prowl. She wondered
if he was headed for a rendezvous, or only hoped for a
chance encounter in the aimless flow of energy on the
streets of town. She thought of Julie's young smoothness
and unlocked ardor.

Leona left to beat the darkness home, another year's
picnic behind her, its hot dog and potato salad con-
sumed.

Myra sat near the fire with her back against a log and
they passed among them a mutant kitten that Tom had
persuaded Florence to bring on the trail, carrying it in
her pocket and feeding it warm milk many times a day

from a penicillin syringe. It was a runt, an albino, absurdly frail and weak, with a long, narrow rodent's face and tremendous flaring ears of pink silk. Neal called it Jaws. Tom had found it in the barn, a white feather in the hay, abandoned by its mother, and took it in to Florence. Its piteous meows were the strongest thing about it. Tom held it, blind and splayed in his palm, and knew he could crush the life from it with a gentle squeeze, and yet there it lay in infant tyranny bellowing to be fed, and he obliged. The kitten made gods of them, living by their indulgence, and they loved it as their own creation. Now it passed from hand to hand and clung for warmth against each chest, knitting its tiny transparent claws into fabric.

Arlen wouldn't take it. When he first saw it he had pushed it away, his face curled in sadness and disgust, and he went to sit in the hayloft with a can of store-bought cat food calling, "Kitty, kitty, kitty," in a strained falsetto until the cats came, their tails straight up, already purring. Then Arlen snatched up the males one by one, last year's kittens, and plunged them head first into a gunny sack in his lap and clamped them between his knees while he nipped out the testicles with his pocketknife.

Myra came upon him surrounded by the miasma of mackerel scent and the swarm of cats. He looked up. "It got by me last year. They breed their mothers. It's sick to save that cat. The mother knew. She carried it out of the nest. It's not meant to live."

"It wants to live," said Myra, thinking of its blind scrabble, cold in the hay. But now, holding it and feeling it thrusting under her chin in an insistent requisition for succor, she suddenly pulled it from her shirt like a burr and handed it on to Tom. Could it live and grow and mate, tenacious and deformed progenitor of a new race?

Tom's blunt finger, thick as the kitten's neck, stroked it, and Bonnie lay against him and watched its progress up his shirt. Myra felt with Tom Bonnie's teasing

warmth and weight, the soft lump of her breast against
his arm and her breath on his neck, and hated her for it,
taking smug possession of him before her eyes, and not
paying the price later in the darkness, but going inside
the trailer to sleep under her father's eye, chaste
daughter, while Tom lay beneath the trailer like a dog
and listened to its shifting weight as she turned in her
sleep. But Tom's eyes were as blank as black marbles
when they rolled toward Myra.

Florence went into the trailer and rattled around,
doing the dishes she couldn't burn, and putting things
away. Arlen unhitched the pickup and drove up the road
to see what the cows were doing. The fire collapsed in
on itself, its light and warmth gone, and Myra went to
bed.

All night through her dreams she heard a horse
stamping its irritation, tied up short and high to a tree,
unable to graze, and the earth beneath her ear
telegraphed the halting steps of a hobbled horse as it
grazed unseen in the darkness so close Myra pictured its
prehensile lip working toward her across the short grass,
and its teeth, square and solid as Mahjong tiles, looming
before her face.

It was almost dawn when Neal came back. He cut his
lights and coasted in to a stop, but Myra woke. She lay
curled in her sleeping bag, her back against a willow,
away from the trailer and the logs of John's boys, and
watched. He'd been home—there was enough light to
make out the neon roses splashed across a dress shirt.
He walked off down the road, weaving, carrying his
rope. He'd be going to bring up the rest of the horses
left behind in a half-section pasture of George Hughes's.
She hadn't seen his face.

When it was lighter and the trailer shuddered with
activity, and Myra was up, she walked past Neal's pickup
and saw her cigarettes lying on the seat. She reached a
hand in the open window and laid it on the cardboard
solidness, oh, the wealth of a whole carton, the security,
and the exultation of having remained in his mind—a

double gift. But she didn't take it; as long as it remained in his possession a part of her was with him.

They started again before breakfast in a dense ground fog that lay across the land in a knee-deep blanket. The horses arched their necks and looked in wonder for their feet, feeling for the vanished earth. They wound into a canyon, strung out miles long like an eerie, improbable, dark current alongside the turbulent La Bonte, slim origin of their river at home. Florence honked through, sending the cattle plunging up the sidehills and scattering into the willow thickets along the creek. She handed bacon and egg sandwiches and gulps of scalding coffee from a thermos out through the window.

At mid-morning the walls of the canyon fell away into swampy willow flats, blue with wild iris like cloud shadows on the sedge, and Arlen counted the cattle through the last fence before the country opened up between spreading wings of ridges. Wide fingers of aspen followed the drainages out of the hills, their branches gray, leaves yet unfurled here where winter clung. The fog was gone and steam rose from the ground and from the drying wool of Neal's jacket.

They nooned there although it was still early. Myra gave the dogs her sandwich behind the trailer so Florence wouldn't see, and drank thin coffee and ate a Milky Way standing in the mud of the road with Neal and Tom, watching the cows spread further and further in all directions.

"They do that every year," said Neal, "It's hell gathering them up again, but still, it's the only place to stop."

Florence came out with the coffeepot and refilled their cups, her free arm clamped across her chest. "Don't you want to come in where it's warmer?" she asked.

"There's no room in there," said Neal for all of them.

Florence looked back toward the canyon's rocky walls on the other side of the cattleguard. "In a month those sidehills'll be covered with moss roses," she said. Myra looked back too, picturing it, and marveling that Florence should ever have noticed such a thing, or expressed it now. In her mind the canyon walls flamed with color.

Riding was hard after the cattle spilled into the open rangeland, always at a trot or a lope, up and back, up and back, along a section of the herd, counteracting the sideways spreading of the cattle, whooping and shouting, trying to maintain the forward motion. It was like trying to contain water. The cattle spilled out every crack, seeming to develop a devious intelligence governed by their greed for the upland grasses. Their lowered heads swung in hasty arcs snatching mouthfuls while their eyes rolled in watchfulness at the approaching rider, waiting until the last minute before fading back into the herd. The moment the rider passed the cattle bulged out again, heads down and feasting.

The land rolled toward the horizon between bedrock ridges in low swells that the line of cattle crawled across in slow undulations like a torpid snake. From her perspective in the drag Myra could watch the toy riders ahead in their monotonous looping, effort erased by distance.

Tom left them the next morning. Myra couldn't think when he'd done it—he must have caught John Bell passing on the road. He'd hired on for the summer to fence and ride colts and put up the native hay. He was saddling up beside Arlen in the early light when she heard him say, "I talked to John Bell?" Making it a question. Arlen looked at him, hearing something in his tone. "He said he could use me this summer, so I guess I'm quitting after we get out to the pasture."

Arlen stiffened and Myra's pulse beat in her ears while she watched him jerk his cinch a hole tighter, then swing up. He looked down at Tom and shook his head. "No," he said, his voice icy, "You're fired. We'll get out to the pasture without you, but don't come whining around next fall looking for work, pleading family. I'm not having you back on my place," and he spun his horse away.

Tom looked across his horse's withers at Myra and grinned a little as he stripped the saddle off. "Well, 'bye, Ma," pricking her with a sliver of rejection. He backed the horse away from the fence and slipped the bridle from its head and it trotted off, leaving nothing between them but their own walls and defenses.

Myra reached to kiss him. "'Bye, Tom. I hope you make out okay. Come see me."

Tom grinned. "When A.D. cools down."

Myra mounted and looked down at him. His face was a rough and pasty moon, his eyes down-turned crescents, and his grin showed his father's small, spaced teeth. He could be on a street corner just as easily she guessed, and she was glad she was leaving him here, with his saddle at his feet and the wind chasing high, pink clouds eastward. He'd be out of work in the fall when John Bell went back to Laramie to break colts and wait out the winter. She wondered as she spurred her horse away that she didn't feel more loss.

Florence leaned out the trailer door and called shrilly, "Tom, come in here," and when he did she said, "Sit down here and drink a cup of coffee while I clean up. I've got to go up to Bell's to get water and you might as well ride up there with me as walk." Tom smiled at her. "He'll get over it," she said. "Probably if you come around next year, if you're out of work, he'll put you on."

When the cattle were moving out of the pasture where they'd been held for the night, Tom went out and hitched the trailer to the pickup for Florence and slipped the stabilizing jacks from under its corners. The herd filed by, bunched and quiet. Arlen sat his horse at the pasture gate counting, and when the last of the cattle were through he loped ahead. He didn't glance at Tom as he passed.

It was disorienting to be standing there watching them go without him, and Tom wondered if he'd done what he wanted. He knew what lay ahead for them, could picture the plains lying out beyond the level pale line of the western horizon—it was the landscape of memory for him, where he'd started his days, more vast and empty and promising less in his mind's eye than it might if he were to ride through it. He threw his saddle into the back of the pickup.

The herd was moving away, and as he watched them becoming distant, Neal detached himself and loped back. Tom walked down the road to meet him, his hands in his pockets, suddenly shy.

Neal reined in and the horse swung around, pulling at the reins, not wanting to be left. "You sure put a burr up A.D.," said Neal, grinning. He knew, looking down at Tom, that he was glad he was going. Their paths had always been bound to diverge, and this was the place. But he knew too that Tom was both more and less than a friend and cousin. They hadn't ever talked much, not even in the darkness of the bunkhouse, or driving the miles home from town together through innumerable nights, drunk, but Neal guessed that, mysterious and un-knowable as they were to each other, they were bound together by love or blood or fate. He envied Tom, think-ing that there was a bend in his road and Tom wouldn't know what lay ahead until he got there, while his own road was as straight and predictable as the road to the plains. Neal got down and put a big pinch of snuff in his lip and gave the can to Tom—a gift to hold him until someone drove to Rock River with a list. Then they smiled at each other and Neal mounted again.

"So long," said Neal.

"See you around," responded Tom, and then Neal was cantering away.

Tom rode beside Florence in the pickup to the Bells. They overtook the herd and pushed through. The kids called out to Tom, "Good-bye! 'Bye, Tom." He lifted his hand but slid his eyes away.

In years past Florence had filled their jugs and tank with the runoff water flowing amber clear through the narrow ditches dissecting the fields of native grasses. It was icy and tasted of snow, but everyone got sick.

The Bell's headquarters was in an elbow right up against the granite outcroppings that winged the valley, a pink-painted, cinder-block house surrounded by the weathered silver of the corrals and barns. A handful of two-year-old colts in the corral milled and circled when Florence drove up. Mrs. Bell was in a patch of mowed prairie in front of the house in her bathrobe, a gopher trap in her hands. She walked over to them and peered distractedly in at Florence without appearing to recognize her.

"Hi, Mrs. Bell," said Florence, "John said we could fill up with water. We didn't want to use the ditch water, it made us all sick last year."

Mrs. Bell murmured, a sound that could be taken as an affirmative, then looked at the trap and said, "These gophers. I can't get rid of them. The dogs won't help. John won't help. I can't see good enough to shoot them. I'm going to trap them."

"Well, yes, they're hard to get rid of, I know," said Florence, but she was already pulling away, moving the trailer up closer to the house within reach of the garden hose. She started laughing as soon as Mrs. Bell's face slid past the window. "I don't think she even knew who I was," she said. "Too many winters up here with John."

The old lady made Tom nervous. She hadn't looked
likely to know anything about him, and there was no
sign of John. He took his saddle out of the pickup and
threw it over the corral fence, then walked around the
trailer to where Florence was standing with the hose.
She pushed it down into the tank where it would stay
by itself and put her arms around Tom and pulled him
close. Her soft plumpness conferred an unexpected
maternal comfort that he couldn't remember ever feeling
in Myra's arms, and he leaned against her and let her
rock him gently from side to side.

"You be good, Tom," Florence said, "You can come
back anytime."

When she let him go Tom wondered if her warmth
now or her daily indifference was more real, but his
eyes stung with tears that he walked away to hide.

When Florence pulled away he was sitting on the
corral fence beside his saddle watching Mrs. Bell setting
gopher traps.

Chapter Seventeen

Myra was riding a borrowed gray horse that played out after six days of hard riding, and at noon she caught a fresh one from the little bunch of extras that traveled with the cattle and were ridden in rotation. She unsaddled the gray and watched him drift off grazing. He had belonged to a Bible thumper who had run a drug rehabilitation camp outside of town. One night at the railroad crossing at Orin just off the interstate he'd stalled his pickup on the tracks in the path of an oncoming freight. He'd gotten out in time but the engine caught the front end of the truck and slammed it around on top of him, and no one knew who claimed ownership of the horse now. Arlen had heard about it and sent Myra and Neal southeast of town to find it and borrow it for the trail. They found it pastured with a brown mare beside the old highway. They had oats and a halter but as soon as the truck and trailer pulled to a stop outside the fence the brown mare cantered away, not waiting to be entrapped by the seductive lure of a shaken oats bucket, and the gelding shadowed her like a colt. Neal and Myra had to unhitch the trailer and run the horses through the pasture with the pickup, careening through the sage, until they

pinned them in a corner and Neal roped the gray. Myra
sat on the tailgate and led him back to the trailer behind
the truck, the mare trotting alongside, nickering her
anxiety, already projecting the coming loneliness.

It was late afternoon before Myra thought to look for
him again and he wasn't with the other loose horses.
She loped along the herd looking hopefully among
them, but he wasn't there, and when she came up to
Arlen he told her to watch for a passing car and hitch a
ride back to look for him—he might never turn up if he
was left to drift alone. Myra thought of him grazing back
along the way they'd come, longing for the brown mare
left neighing at the fence.

She watched the road anxiously—sometimes whole
days would pass with hardly a car—but within an hour
the cattle were parting for a red Bronco, and Myra
squeezed into the backseat with her saddle behind two
fat ladies. As they were pulling away a relay of shouts
from the riders arrested them. Neal was galloping down
the edge of the herd toward them. He slid to a stop and
dismounted and tied the reins in a snug knot up behind
his horse's ears and turned him loose. He climbed into
the car beside Myra and smiled. "I've got to go back for
the pickup."

It seemed a long way they'd come since morning as
they wound back into the hills to the abandoned pickup.
Thigh against thigh, out of the wind in the dusty, sun-
warmed backseat, the saddle enveloping them in the
smell of leather and sweat-soaked wool. The ladies chattered and questioned and Neal answered gravely. Neal's
presence bombarded Myra. She kept her eyes fastened
on his hand where it rested in a relaxed curl against the
frayed denim of his jeans, but when she flashed a glance
at him he was smiling at her out of the sides of his eyes.
She was having trouble catching her breath.

Afterward it had the quality of a dream recollected, a
dream lived so many times in imagination, matched by

reality, that sometimes she couldn't be certain it wasn't a dream.

She could not bear to part with him now. She didn't look at him but saw in her imagination astonishment and disbelief cross his face if she said what was in her mind, and then the quick calculation that moved him past suspicion and into a stunned delight.

So, she laid her hand against his side in the warm intimacy beneath his arm, standing in the road beside the pickup in the settling dust as the Bronco retreated into distance, and it took nothing more than that, and her asking, "Will you walk up into the hills with me?", looking at him now, and his face was as she imagined. She was struck by the whiteness of his eyes. There was a pulse beating at the base of his throat. He bent and picked her saddle up from where it lay at her feet and threw it into the bed of the pickup, then he took her hand and they walked without speaking across the marshy bottom, blue with iris, and up among the granite and grass and aspen.

She touched him with wonder, sweet foreign land, her hands pushing away his shirt, lips and tongue and teeth learning his terrain, arch of bone and plane of flesh, and Neal turned his head away and moaned. Myra felt through his skin, with his nerves, as her hands and mouth played over him, and she lost her body's boundaries against him.

Here winter was never completely gone from the air, but they were sheltered from the wind, and the sun had warmed last year's curled, brown grasses beneath them. The moment was lived through, and gone, and could only be captured in memory—the present moved into the future—and Neal leaned above her, his eyes prodigal with tenderness, and Myra fended off words of hope and promise—oh, to remain in the perfect communication of wordless cries and whispers.

Myra sat up and buttoned her jeans. Looking at him she thought she could go again—he stopped her breath—but the horse was back on her mind. She stood up and looped the bridle over her shoulder and looked down at him, then she was walking away and he had to hurry to catch her as she mounted the ridge until from the top she could look for miles in all directions. The wind was strong here, and the sun hung lower, stretching their shadows. The happy luxury of the afternoon faded, replaced by the urgency of the need to find the horse and return.

Her eyes scanned the plains and Neal watched her. "We could just not go back," he said, and for a moment she was hightailing it like a bandit through the canyon with him in the dark, sitting close against his arm. But then she caught sight of some dark shapes miles up the valley toward Bell's, and a lighter one with them, and she was pointing.

"There, I'll bet that's him," she said. They looked together, fixing the location in their minds, squinting through the distance. She almost could go with him, empty his savings account and rattle into North Dakota on back roads on a diet of beer and Cheetos. Hire on somewhere together. Leave the horse grazing eastward with new companions, and plunge into the suspended reality of the road, outrunning squalor.

But as she turned to him, lips parted in assent, he said, "Let's go get him," and started down the shoulder of the ridge ahead of her.

They found him two miles up the road, off in the wet bottomland grazing with a little band of mares. The ground was too wet for the pickup and Myra and Neal were soaked by the time Neal finally got a loop on him.

Standing beside the pickup in the slanting light Myra looked at Neal and longed to hold him again, to bring back the afternoon, but she grinned at him as though it hadn't been, and mounted and loped away with a tearless ache in her chest. She supposed, she hoped, that she'd given him something she'd never feel again herself.

It gave her solace to think that he would carry her in his memory for all of his life, as she'd carried his father, and that in that small way she would never age or perish. She let the horse slow to a shuffling trot that would eat up the miles, and the pickup passed on the road in a cloud of dust, light and fast, traveling on the tops of the washboard. She saw Neal's quick glance in her direction before his eyes were again on the road, and the pickup continued and was gone, and she was alone.

Chapter Eighteen

When Myra rode away and left Neal standing by the pickup without a look or a touch to give him the gift of her continuing intimacy, he shook his head. It might never have been. But he could still feel her teeth in his shoulder and her legs gripping his ribs.

He covered the miles in minutes and came upon the dragging tail of the herd and honked through. She would be hours behind him. He ignored the waving figure of his father trying to flag him at the head of the herd, and drove on by and down the road to where they would spend the night. It was still a mile to go and he could tell the cows had quit moving and the riders would be fighting them. Florence came out of the trailer and climbed into the truck beside him, and he turned around and drove back. She was worried and nagged in her cracked voice, "God, Neal, what took you so long? A.D.'s fit to be tied." But Neal didn't answer. Vincent had caught his horse and came to meet them. The sun had fallen below the western horizon and the herd was lowing and the dust hung in the evening lull, but the noise and surroundings fell away when Arlen approached and looked at him. Their eyes locked. Neal

saw the accusation on his father's face fade into an
angry uncertainty. Arlen would watch him now with
new eyes and they would do battle in another arena.
Neal mounted his horse and spun him away.

Neal rode that night in a slowly repeating quarter circle
around the herd, holding it loosely bunched against a
fence. The herd was restless, there had been no water
since morning and the cows were thirsty. The calves
that had found their mothers got little comfort from the
shrunken bags, and bawled on, hoarsely complaining.
The cows bawled too, and paired up slowly, and many
stood at the edge of the herd, facing out, yearning
homeward. Neal thought how stupid the cows were,
and how stupidly crafty. They wouldn't learn. They had
no judgment or imagination and would try over and
over to elude him, breaking out of the herd and heading
off. To where? Stupid old rips, your calves are here. Just
look. And if you think you're thirsty now, wait until
tomorrow. He was tired but knew he wouldn't sleep,
and after two hours he didn't go in for a replacement
but rode on, his thoughts on Myra. He knew she had
come in. He'd seen her on the road as she came up, a
ghost on the gray horse. He wondered if she were sleeping now, and if she thought of him. Having had her,
having wrapped his arms around her and having felt her
beneath him, she remained unattainable. He knew he'd
go on looking at her with longing, contriving to be close
to her. It was a cruel jest of fate to put in his path a
woman he would so desire but couldn't even try to win.
If you could warp time, he thought, so their lives could
touch in a different place, it would be all right for them
both. He looked up, the wind on his face, into the dizzy-
ing depths of the stars and wondered, if you died, did
you range through time?

The sorting was done at the gates in the intersecting fence lines on the top of the vast, featureless, undulating planet of short grass stretching to the curve of the earth. A final marathon day on horseback, gathering and holding and cutting, dividing the cattle among the four pastures. Now the cattle were spreading away in an expanding circle—dark shapes like a random pattern of shot scattering across the plains.

The wind dropped. The dust settled. No one broke the quiet. They closed the gates and led the tired horses to the pickups and pulled off the saddles and the horses moved off slowly, as though doubting their liberty. Myra threw her saddle into the back of Neal's pickup with the others and climbed on top of the load and leaned back in the topography of the tack. The kids and dogs piled in. Neal leaned into the cab and took a half-empty bottle of Canadian from the seat and drank, and handed her the bottle with a look she couldn't read, and she took a cautious sip. She rolled it around on her tongue and drank again and handed it on to Bonnie.

Neal got in and started the truck and the horses diminished behind them in a cloud of dust. The bottle went all the way around the back of the pickup. Myra thought that the idea alone was making the kids high, and they surely didn't like the taste. The boys wiped their lips with the backs of their hands and exhaled in surprise. The bottle came back to Myra and she leaned out over the side and handed it in through the window to Neal. She caught her breath when their fingers brushed as the bottle passed, and their eyes met for a moment in the sideview mirror before his image vibrated away. Myra watched his arm as it alternately lay along the window, his fingers curled around the neck of the bottle, and rose to take a pull. She was aroused by the unconscious loveliness of this piece of him—delicate bones articulating beneath brown skin—and in her mind her fingers ran along the raised tracings of veins. She could feel the whiskey.

When they pulled to a stop beside the trailer where it was parked by the windmill and water tank Neal turned the radio up loud and the song wailed out, all its volume a small thing against the wind, carried away like a shout. Neal took Myra's hand to steady her when she jumped down from the bed of the pickup and while the boys unloaded the saddles, watching with furtive, embarrassed glances, he waltzed with her in the dust. He held her away from him, dipping and gliding under the pearl sky on top of the plains. Myra wished they could whirl on, spinning into distance, but the song ended and Neal dropped his arms and walked back to the truck. He got in alone and leaned against the door looking like he was settling down to finish the bottle by himself. He hadn't spoken a word. Arlen was watching from the trailer door and the boys looked at her out of troubled eyes. She picked up her saddle and leaned it against the side of the trailer on its pommel with spread skirts to dry the sweat.

Arlen stayed behind to ride the fence lines with a bundle of metal posts and a roll of wire in the back of the truck when the others returned home, all of them piled into Neal's pickup, winding back along the way they'd come, whipping past landmarks still fresh with the intimacy of their slow passage. Arlen liked the trailer now the congestion of rolled sleeping bags and Hefty sacks filled with dirty socks and jeans was gone, and the lineup of muddy boots on newspapers no longer tripped him at the door. He read an old Max Brand over twice-daily meals of bacon and eggs. At night he lay in the trailer in the dark while the wind nudged and moaned outside, a presence he would have missed if it had died. He didn't think. His mind rode the wind around the trailer, exploring the loose corners of aluminum siding, caught in torn screening, then flowing eastward in an uninterrupted sweep. The curtain billowed, then sucked tight against the screen, and he studied the patterns in the wallpaper in the darkness. He was cleansed by the universe of grass and sky and ungoverned by his pre-occupations. He could have stayed content on the plains all summer, fixing fence, tinkering with the windmills, and chugging out among the cattle at sundown as they congregated around the tanks. The calves bucked in the evening coolness on the surrounding green grass cropped close as a fairway, happy to be alive, and Arlen wondered where it was that happiness fled.

Chapter Nineteen

The horses flung up their heads at the approach of the pickup, and startled away, then turned like curious antelope and watched. Then they were flying away in an unweighted gallop ahead of the truck until Neal and Myra and Vincent ran them into a corner of the pasture and pinned them there with lariat ropes strung across the open end of the angle of the fences. It was a week later and Arlen had sent them back out to the plains with the six-horse trailer to retrieve the Glendo horses and three of his own. They were hurrying because big, roiling, flat-bottomed thunderheads were crowding the northern sky. The powdery silt that clung among the sparse grass would turn to gumbo with the rain and they'd never be able to haul the trailer out. But when they had loaded the horses and coiled the ropes back up and hung them behind the seat on the rifle rack Neal said, "I want to find Clay." Myra looked at the remaining loose horses. She hadn't noticed that Clay wasn't among them.

"Geez, Neal," said Vincent, "we'll never get out of here." Neal grinned and got into the pickup and drove out from under the gooseneck and Vincent had to scramble to catch up and climb into the cab. They drove up a gradual shoulder that rose so gently that even from its highest point it didn't give much vantage. A solitary horse could easily be hidden in a distant fold of hill. Neal continued at random, remaining on the ridges when he could, eyes scanning the surrounding plains.

They found him finally in the northeast corner. They were suddenly upon him—the dark shape had seemed much further away because he was down, wrapped and entangled, caught in the fence. His head was up, supported by the wire.

Neal got out and approached him. No quiver of fear this time, no bunching of muscles ready to spring away, just stillness. In the center of his forehead where a cowlick had been there was a tidy bullet hole. Neal didn't go to him. He stopped as he always had, giving him a little space, not crowding him. He'd never catch him now. The wire was embedded deep into his hide, and the coyotes had been at him. Neal looked north into the hills. The shelf of clouds was almost upon them. The grass at his feet bent softly eastward under the memory of the wind. Neal looked back at Clay. His head was angled inquiringly backward over his shoulder as though for a final glance at life as he left it. His struggle was over, the thudding heartbeat stilled. He wouldn't feel the rain, or the coyotes rending, at rest out here on the plains. Myra and Vincent came up to stand beside Neal, awed by his loss.

"He's not hurt that bad," said Neal finally, "they should have cut him free. They didn't even try."

"Who do you suppose it was?" asked Vincent, and a picture leapt into Myra's mind of Arlen, holding the rifle hip-high in one hand like a pistol and shooting with fatal, careless marksmanship, the gun leaping as the shell exploded, killing more than a horse, killing a spark that refused to capitulate, and she sobbed once at the image. She wondered if it could have been, and searched Neal's face.

"I don't know," said Neal, as though it didn't matter, and he went to the pickup and got the fencing pliers from the dashboard and came back and knelt beside Clay. He cut the wire, snipping it into short lengths, until the horse's head dropped heavily onto his arm and he laid it flat on the ground. Then he moved around the body, cutting and untangling, lifting the embedded wire from deep canyons in Clay's taut haunches, unwinding it from slim, brown, cannon bones. When he was done he and Vincent spliced the fence back together above the horse with wire from the truck.

The wind came up before they were done, bringing the rain and sweeping it southward in almost horizontal sheets. When the fence was repaired the three of them stood in a ragged, solemn semicircle around the dead horse. They were soaked to the skin, their clothes plastered against them. "Jesus, I'm frozen," said Vincent, and he went back to the pickup and climbed in. Myra looked at Neal. She thought he must feel grief, but his face showed nothing and she wasn't sure—were tears concealed by the rain on his cheeks? They turned and went back to the truck and slid in. Neal reached across Myra and found a pint of Four Roses in the glove box, and they passed it back and forth while the rain sheeted the windshield and Clay lay dark and blurred beyond.

Neal didn't want to leave. He relived coming upon Clay, before the rain, taking slow steps toward him as his breath whooshed in his nostrils and he struggled against the wire. Neal murmured as he approached, and at the last moment before his hand touched the horse's neck, Clay bent forward to meet him, then lay quiet as Neal cut the wire until he was free to lurch to his feet and stand without restraint while Neal explored the extent of his injuries. But crowding in over this came the nightmare image of the horse thrashing wildly, heaving himself against the binding wire at the approach of a faceless figure. The shot rang out in Neal's mind, the flat, powerful explosion of a rifle at close range, and Clay sagged into the fence. Neal thought of Clay lying

forever like an equine Prometheus while the coyotes
shredded his flesh, and he suddenly slid out of the pickup and hurried to cup one palm over the horse's nostril
and to lay his other hand flat behind Clay's elbow. He
hunched in the rain for long minutes to be convinced
that there was no whisper of breath or heart.

Neal got back into the truck and drove away, but circled
around after a while to a hilltop where he got out and
squinted through the rain. His heart leapt—had Clay
risen? Had he wandered off? But then he saw the fence
line and the dark shape lying beneath it.

They found the horse trailer in the downpour and
hooked on and snaked along through the mud in spurts
until they were brought to a halt by a rise that the truck
couldn't climb. And there they sat, jackknifed in deep,
red ruts, while the storm fled southward. The bellies of
the clouds were pink and gold and mauve, lit by the
departed sun, and the prairies stretched away into darkness.

"The wind'll suck the rain right up out of the mud
and we'll get out in the morning," said Neal. The light
faded, the Four Roses was gone, and Vincent leaned
against the window and slept.

Myra studied the side of Neal's face, and he must
have felt her gaze for a long time before he turned and
looked at her with heavy-lidded eyes, crescents of white
beneath the blue irises. Myra's hand flew up to cradle his
cheek as he bent to kiss her and she arched against him
in a wordless offer to slip outside and lean up against
the fender and let him inside her—an urgent thrusting
union to dispel despair—but he stopped kissing her as
suddenly as he had begun, his arm draped across her
shoulders, and the wall was back over his eyes, screening him from her even when he smiled. "Let's go to
Rock River," he said. She thought he was kidding until
he got out and unhitched the horse trailer again, and
then gunned the pickup out from under the gooseneck

and slid uphill in low gear with the pedal on the floor. Vincent woke up and slowly digested this turn of events. He looked back and saw they were trailerless, and looked around Myra to Neal. "It's Saturday night, kid—we're going to town," said Neal.

"Rock River?" asked Vincent, and grinned with groggy pleasure when Neal nodded.

It took a long time to get to the county road. They were stuck more than once and Myra and Vincent sat on the tailgate in a storm of sprayed gumbo and bounced their weight for traction while the tires spun and the engine whined. It would have been a lark if it hadn't been for Myra's uneasy feeling that a stranger inhabited Neal. He acted as he normally would, and smiled and spoke, but as though by remembered conventions. She entertained the odd fancy that they had died and were ghosts haunting the dark plains on roads leading nowhere. Was the spirit of Clay galloping, floating over wire? Did she hear the light drumroll of his hooves?

The lights of Rock River rose in the distance. A wide spot straddling old U.S. 30 and the Union Pacific tracks—home once, the center of her universe. The faded, chrome yellow shacks where the road gangs once stayed were boarded up and surrounded by a high mesh fence. Plywood had been nailed over the ground floor glass of the hotel but upstairs a panel of white net flapped limply out a paneless window. Myra knew the room, could picture the wallpaper and the view of the street. She might have hung the curtain years ago, washed and starched and pressed, looking down upon the roof of Arlen's pickup parked in front of the bar where she now sat.

Heads turned as they walked in. Myra looked down the long, narrow room at the remembered advertising neon and dark wood and the horror of the two-headed calf, and she recognized a few of the faces along the bar. Then swimming up at her from the depths of the mirror came Tom's face. It shouldn't have been such a surprise to see him there—Bell's wasn't much further back into the hills than the pasture where they'd come from, but still she hadn't thought to see him again for a while.

They took their drinks and sat with him and the Mexican girl with outlined eyes he didn't introduce.

"How're you doing?" asked Neal.

"Getting by," said Tom.

Myra fed two dollars worth of quarters into the jukebox and took her time making her selections—she wished to be anywhere else than sitting across from Tom with Neal's knee nudging hers under the table. Some of the tunes were the same ones she had played when the hotel was hers, before the interstate, when transcontinental traffic still passed through town, and a stranger might stop for a beer and a room and biscuits and gravy for breakfast. Rock River had seemed like a starting place. Myra felt light and insubstantial as though she was a memory drifting in someone else's thoughts.

Neal and Tom drank boilermakers with steady intensity, buying alternate rounds as though seeing and raising each other at cards. Tom talked about John Bell's colts, and the old man's memories—stories of Tom Horn and blizzards—and Neal tilted his chair back and draped his arm around Myra's shoulders with his fingers inside her collar brushing the hollow of her throat. Vincent went to sleep. The Mexican girl ordered sloe screws and kept her hand down under the table between Tom's legs.

Toward closing time Tom put both hands palm down on the table with his fingers spread and leaned across to Neal. "You mother fucker," he said. Silence, as he stared. Then he half stood and reached to flip Neal's arm from Myra's shoulder. "You're fucking my mother." Myra's head spun and she had to grip the edge of the table to keep from sliding to the floor. Neal was white around the lips and standing up, kicking his chair backward. Tom laughed, then said, "Outside," through clenched teeth.

They walked away from her, down the length of the bar, shoulder to shoulder, and she watched their retreating figures as though through the wrong end of binoculars.

Myra went out through the back with Vincent and stood in the alley and held his head while he vomited. She could hear the fight out front—distant scuffling and grunts, and the encouragement from the onlookers who had followed them out. She saw the fists and faces in her imagination, and held her breath for teeth and noses. Her palm supported Vincent's damp forehead, and she looked up and let herself spiral away into the stars beyond her shame.

A long while later they walked through the alley and out into the deserted street to find the pickup—where else was there to go?— and surrendered to the anesthetic of sleep. Later still Neal got in beside her. Myra woke and remembered and looked at him in anguish for their disgrace and for the mess of his face and hands.

She had never thought of this, of discovery, of consequence and responsibility, other people's perceptions. Her desire had pushed perspective away to the ends of her consciousness until her total reality was lived in the moment. The desire, which had seemed pure in its intensity and fundamental in its consummation, now appeared perverse and defiling. But still she longed to touch him, to lift his hand from the steering wheel and suck the pain from his swollen knuckles.

Dawn was breaking in a thin line above the eastern hills when they got back to the trailer. The horses inside whinnied at their approach. Neal slid out and Myra followed him, and in a moment Vincent staggered out into the dawn and slowly took things in through the fog of his first hangover. "What happened?" he asked finally, looking at Neal's face.

"I got in a fight," said Neal and his eyes flicked Myra's for the barest instant—did Vincent not remember? Might last night's words remain forever between the two of them and Tom?

"Oh," said Vincent, and he walked around the truck to pee, and when he came back buttoning his pants he asked, "Tom too?"

"Yeah, Tom too," said Neal. He wound the gooseneck down onto the hitch.

"Who with?" asked Vincent.

Neal looked at him patiently. "With each other. Let's see if we can get out of here."

He pulled around in a wide circle and took a run at the hill and spun up it in mud and smoke. Vincent was holding his head.

Neal said they were driving around, back through Rock River and Bosler and Wheatland because yesterday's rain would have made the canyon impassable, but Myra wondered if there were other reasons. Perhaps he didn't want to pass again the spot by the iris and the finger of aspen. They would feel it approaching, watching the landmarks, living again the miles in the red Bronco in the innocence of their desire before they knew what they were going to do. Then it would be behind them, the place on the road where they'd left the pickup a charged location as where a death has occurred, and they would travel onward until they passed Bell's, and beyond to where Tom left them. But perhaps he thought only of the horses and the thrashing tangle of legs if the trailer should swing wide in the mud of a corner and hang up angled and slanted on the shoulder. Maybe she was out of his thoughts, swept away by the fight, vanquished to memory.

She knew better though, when they passed through Rock River and his face changed color and his hand shook as he shifted gears in front of the bar. East of the town he pulled off into the barrow pit and stood at the back of the pickup, coughing and retching.

"What's wrong?" asked Vincent, and Myra put her arm around him for a moment—soft, unformed, adolescent bulk—then slid out and stood in the promise of the warm, dawn wind. Neal was leaning on his crossed arms against the edge of the pickup bed, his face hidden. A

little band of antelope watched them from a rise in the
pasture across the highway, then flowed out of sight.
Neal raised his head and looked at her.

"Let's go," she said, "You said it yourself. We can
get out of here." Now she was pleading, both hands on
his forearm, looking into his eyes. "It doesn't matter.
Nothing matters. We'll just clear out." She couldn't
understand why he didn't see it. Why he just stood
there staring at her. "Neal," she said, and parted his
shirt at the throat, both hands flat against his chest and
beneath her palm his heart thudded, "let's go." She
knew that by now Vincent was half turned to look out
the back window at them, and she didn't care, but Neal
wasn't listening.

"Oh, God," said Myra. She was helpless to help
him—she didn't even know what might be in his mind.
They had never talked and she had wanted it that way,
had wanted the purity of an unknown being to project
perfection onto, and in whom to read the reflection of
her own desires. She was wicked, unnatural, descending
into Neal's dreams, and he woke to find the nightmare
real. She had no solace of understanding to offer, no
comprehension of the elements of his pain. Their complicity wasn't a bond, for she couldn't guess the focus of
his guilt—the deed itself, the discovery, continuing
desire? He lived alone now in an isolated sea of torment.
There was no answer but forgetfulness, and only time
could achieve that.

They got back into the pickup and drove on. Vincent
slept again. At Bosler they turned east toward Wheatland
on 34 and climbed into the broken hills on a ribbon of
blacktop, and at every turn Myra lived Gene Wells's
wreck in her imagination. She thought of Tom, back out
at Bell's this morning riding colts in the pure light of his
righteousness, the impact of each step jarring his hangover and the bruises on his face.

She had once held a cat, too young a mother, and
she remembered her revulsion when she discovered that
as it lay curled in her lap it sucked from its own tit, con-

suming itself, contented infant and dam to itself, while its kittens mewled in the desolation of their nest. She was such a mother.

As they came down out of the canyon Vincent was awake and wanting to go through Wheatland for tacos. It would have been easier to skirt the town because of the horse trailer, and Neal and Myra couldn't eat, but Neal had a lot of empathy with a hangover.

They stopped in Glendo to drop Vincent and the horses. Leona was sitting in the shade of the porch and called "Hello" to them, her voice sweet and reaching like the fragrance of the honeysuckle climbing to the roof.

"Hi, Grandma," Neal and Vincent called together, boys, and Myra flushed—in a few years then would she be wanting Vincent?

The horses stepped out and shook themselves in the sunlight. Lorraine emerged from the trailer, barefoot, pale, blinking and smoking. "Well, come on in and have a glass of tea," she said.

Neal asked, "Is John around?"

"He's across the crick," said Lorraine, "He should be back by dinner."

Neal stood silently for a long moment, staring off toward the cottonwoods, then he said, "He'll have to get these horses home some way," and spun away from them.

He was already unhitching the trailer when Myra cried, "No!", a plea wrung up and called out as she pulled at his arm. She hadn't thought to lose him so soon. Where was he going? She tried to turn him toward her, tugging at his shoulders. Lorraine was watching with interest. Myra followed him around the pickup and clung to the door as he got in. "Neal," she said, "where are you going?"

He looked at her. "'Bye, Myra," he said, and then he drove away, out of the yard, leaving her in the dust of his going. He gave her no time—no time for tears to rise

up, glazing her eyes and softening his heart, no time for
a kiss and an inquiring tongue persuading him to linger,
no time for a caressing hand promising comfort.

"Well," said Lorraine, "what bit him?" A rhetorical
question. "Come on in. I'll give you a glass of tea."

Myra was trying to think. She could still hear the engine of the pickup fading to a murmur, the last of him,
gone when the truck rounded a bend. She followed Lorraine inside then, moving irrevocably into a new moment and a further loss, already in motion away from
Neal, time already intervening.

Later, over Lorraine's protests, she hitched the horse
trailer to the '61, the pickup they used to feed and
check fence—old and unreliable with fading brakes and
no first gear. She took Ray's horse up the creek and unloaded it in front of the barn, seeing through the back of
her head the corner of the bedroom shade lifted, and
feeling Rosemary's eyes upon her.

Haying was starting and all the way home she was
assaulted by the memories of all her lost summers
brought back by the hot, sweet fragrance of the cut
meadows—smell, that most powerful of conjurers.

Chapter Twenty

Arlen came down when she was just about ready to pull out. He was on horseback and Easter was still wet from the crossing. Myra thought Florence must have seen her drive in alone with the horses in John's '61, and been watching for him. His long, curling, red beard was gone, shaved off in an annual summer ritual at the kitchen table after the trail. Florence wrapped him up to his neck in a sheet and attacked him first with scissors, then moved on to clippers, leaving a band of white around his ears and neck, and released him to shave the final stubble over the bathroom sink. He emerged, pale and sheepish, a stranger to himself and everyone. Now he leaned on the saddle horn, his hands dangling, and looked at Myra—a skinny, long-faced, bat-eared man—and Myra suddenly saw him as nothing other than her own dear cousin, an ordinary man to be pitied and treasured. Her obsession had banished her from that simple truth.

He sighed and looked at her trailer, the chocks gone from under its corners and its weight on the hitch raking the Cadillac into a stationary angle suggestive of speed. "Well," he said, "send an address. We'll owe you wages." Myra looked at him, and laced her fingers into his. "What did you think, Myra, coming here?" he asked finally, but she only shook her head, no longer meeting his eyes.

And so, she thought, this is where it ended. Arlen before her, stripped of his potency as though it never was. And what of Neal? If he stood before her now she would fall to her knees to keep him near, regard him still with velvet eyes. Reality was a web of deceit woven by desire, and transformed in the blink of an eye—a cat's cradle of the mind, one tug and the whole structure shifted. Her reality lay now with Neal, carried along with her heart wherever he hightailed it.

Myra headed south, where she'd never been before, as far as the panhandle of Texas, and crept slowly northward again through the summer with a harvesting crew, endless miles leading nowhere in the air-conditioned cab of a gleaner, distancing her from her past.

She watched for Neal's pickup, imagining him passing her on the highway, glancing her way as he drew parallel, the instant of recognition, the smile, the pleasure—pulling to the shoulder and the moment's hesitation before the embrace. At night in the towns her eyes swept the lineup in front of the bars, searching for Steamboat bucking on a county 13 plate.

No one thought to look for Neal. Florence figured she'd get a call or a card, or he'd rattle in himself with his tail between his legs sometime before Christmas. She was glad really, she knew it was better for him. If he could have known it would have pleased him how much trouble Arlen had finding someone to take his place. By the beginning of haying he had lost all three of his hands and had a string of high school boys buggering up the equipment. It got to be a joke in town, and Arlen fumed.

Arlen found him late in the summer. He was on horseback out on the plains, gathering the cattle to rotate into
the adjoining pasture in a scheme he'd worked out to
get the most out of his grass. He saw the pickup first,
and was not at first alarmed—it was distant against a
fence line and not immediately recognizable as Neal's,
and he rode easily toward it, curious. But before he
knew why, his heart was fluttering in his throat and he
was having trouble catching his breath. He opened and
closed his fist to see if pain or numbness traveled down
his arm. He had an impulse to turn away, to not inves-
tigate, as though he'd never topped the rise and seen the
dark, distant lump of the truck, and he let his horse
circle wide.

Later he didn't know when he knew what he was
going to see—maybe only after he'd seen, but it might
have been lying in his unconscious for minutes or
forever, the picture of a destiny he'd always been
moving toward. At any rate it was without surprise that
he gazed down at the rags and hide that had been Neal.
It was the hands that were most eloquent, and the teeth,
retaining their integrity within the diminishing flesh,
evoking Neal. Teeth that grimaced skyward and hands in
loose, bewildered curls. The rifle lay along his body, the
stock between his boots, and the stick he had used to
push the trigger. He had sagged backward into the fence
wire.

Arlen didn't get down. The horse braced itself and
nodded a tensed neck, ears pricked, while it blew suspi-
ciously through distended nostrils. The wind teased a
corner of tattered shirttail. Arlen raised his eyes.

The land was parceled up and leased to the neighbors
until it sold. The cattle never came home. They were
shipped straight off the plains, loaded into stock trucks,
and hauled in a dust-plumed convoy to Laramie.
Florence got a job at the drive-up window at the First
National, and an apartment with Bonnie in town. Arlen

moved over to Valerie Pruitt's and sleepwalked through his days.

Events that might have happened anyway—Arlen's debt was so immense—but internalized and lived again with tortured remorse.

It was a long time before Myra learned, and by then the layers of daily living had built up between her and her memories, but even so she stopped him. She wouldn't let go of his arm, and twisted inside it and clamped herself against him and sank her tongue into his mouth until he responded, alive again, with his hand low on her back, fingers slipping inside the waistband of her jeans—on and on while blood returned and thoughts tingled back to life, biting each other's lips with smiles, and kisses on the throat. They left Vincent behind in the dawn, sitting on the fender of the horse trailer with his head in his hands, and drove south together.

Myra didn't give up looking at the faces in passing traffic, but had to ask after every glance, who was it she still sought?